Janet
of Laurel Hill

GENEVIEVE FOX COLLECTION

By Genevieve Fox

First published in 1941

Originally entitled "Green Treasure"

Cover design by Tina DeKam

Cover art by Embla Granqvist

Illustrations by Forrest W. Orr

This unabridged version has updated grammar and spelling.

© 2019 Jenny Phillips

www.thegoodandthebeautiful.com

Contents

I. Berries to Burn 1
II. A Buggy Ride 8
III. Blackberries Are Cheap 17
IV. Mysterious Cousins 21
V. Janet Blows Off Steam 26
VI. In the Good Old Summertime 30
VII. Treasure in the Woods 34
VIII. Janet Gets a Letter 39
IX. The Jersey Heifer 43
X. The Cattle Show 47
XI. "Keep Off" 56
XII. Too Good to Be True 61
XIII. The Big Blow 65
XIV. What the Wind Did 71
XV. Acting a Difficult Part 76
XVI. Christmas on Laurel Hill 80
XVII. A Woodshed Warming 89
XVIII. The Telegram Was Important 96
XIX. Return of a Gold Miner 103
XX. Up a Dead-End Road 110
XXI. Dog in the Manger 116

XXII. Just Like a Picnic	124
XXIII. The Hill's Afire	130
XXIV. Janet Regrets	138
XXV. Janet is Eighteen	144
XXVI. Stephen Loses His Memory	152
XXVII. Old Home Day	159
XXVIII. Janet Forgets Her Speech	164
XXIX. "You've Grown Up, Janet"	172
XXX. Stephen Changes His Mind	177

Chapter 1

Berries to Burn

"Here's your dinner pail, Molly. Have you got a clean handkerchief? Wait a minute. Let me fix your hair."

The tall girl bent down, lifted the wide-brimmed sailor hat from the little girl's head, rearranged the dark curls, replaced the hat, pushed the elastic back under the small chin, and kissed the grave, childish face raised to hers. "Now run along, or you'll be late."

"Goo'bye, Janet. Wish I was all through school and could stay at home and have fun forever and ever like you can," Molly called back as she ran out of the yard.

At these words, Janet Bradley's cheeks flamed, and her bright eyes turned from brown to black. For an instant, she looked as if she were going to run after the small, pinafored figure and shake it. "Just you wait till you're almost sixteen and see if it's fun to stay at home and do the housework and grow up into an ignoramus," she said bitterly. "Anyway, I'm not through school. I'm *not*."

The black-and-white shepherd dog lying on the sunny doorstone backed up her statement by thumping his plumy tail vigorously. The girl knelt and patted the dog's white nose then whispered into one silky ear, "You understand how I feel, don't you, Dick?"

She stood up, half-opened the screen door into the kitchen, then let it slam shut as she looked out to the green hillside rising gradually from the barn to the dark woods on the upper slopes of Laurel Hill. In a second, she was on the other side of the gate in the stone wall and had started along a footpath through the tall grass. Dick bounded ahead, pleased to have an excuse for visiting woodchuck holes. The girl's glance rested with satisfaction on the fattening sides of three calves staked out behind the barn and on the great square of brown earth where rows of dark green rosettes gave promise of early potatoes. Not till she came to the acre-size strawberry patch in the upper lot did she stop. Then, kneeling down on the straw between two rows of plants, she uttered an "Oh-h-h" of delight. "There are going to be just slathers of berries—berries to burn," she said to herself.

Two weeks ago, when the blossoms had lain like a fall of snow on this hillside, her hopes had soared high. Yet, at that time, fear was mixed with hope—fear of a late frost. Even later, when tiny green nubs had formed, there was still danger of too wet or too dry weather. Now plump, greenish-white fruit hung in heavy clusters. One or two big beauties already showed faint pinkish cheeks.

A smile lovely to see spread over Janet's face. No one else could possibly know what the sight of those loaded strawberry plants meant to her. They were not just ripening berries. They were ripening plans for going back to high school next fall. Fortunately, she did not notice how hard-baked the earth was beneath the plants or that the tips of a few berries were dried-up and brown.

All things seemed possible this June morning as Janet hurried down through the fields to the ancient, almost paintless farmhouse. She sang as she washed the breakfast dishes—sang and did mental arithmetic—to the cheerful accompaniment of the teakettle humming through its black iron nose and the singing of bobolinks on the hillside. Last year, they had cleared about forty dollars on strawberries. This year, there must be twice as many plants, with the new bed bearing. Twice forty was eighty. Then, say they cleared forty dollars on red raspberries. And, if Papa had potatoes before anybody else did, he would get a good price for them. Suppose—just suppose they could put three hundred dollars into the bank this summer!

"If the crops do well next year, we'll hire Etta Hastings to keep house in the fall so that you can go back to school," Papa had said again and again last winter. That was such a big "if" on a New England farm, but now it really looked as though he could say that soon, without any "if."

A little more than six months ago, life had been different in the old house on the side of Laurel Hill. Janet had been a carefree girl instead of the "leetle lady of the house," as the tin peddler put it. She had been going back and forth on the train to Eastbrook along with the other Glenbrook boys and girls and having good times, instead of keeping house and trying to be mother to a little sister. Then—in the space of two months—everything was changed.

In December, Janet had stayed out of school to nurse her mother. Through January she stayed out of school to run the house while her mother was in the hospital. After that—after her mother's death—she kept on staying out of school because there were doctor's bills and hospital bills and funeral expenses to pay and no more money to hire a housekeeper.

When the dishes were done, the girl went to the sitting-room cupboard and took down a pile of books from a shelf. Each was covered with manila paper and bore the inscription "Property of the Town of Eastbrook." For a while, she had tried by studying at home to keep up with her class. Soon she had found herself beyond her depth in Caesar, geometry, and beginner's French, without anyone to help her, but she had gone on with her English and had even written compositions to be criticized and corrected by herself.

Propping *The Merchant of Venice* up on the ironing board, she began to read aloud as she ironed her father's shirts. She would study hard all this summer. Then maybe she could do two years' work in one and graduate with her own class. She began to read—

> "The quality of mercy is not strain'd,
> It droppeth as the gentle rain from heaven
> Upon the place beneath. It is twice bless'd:"

A step sounded on the back porch. Old Mr. Matthews, who lived a half a mile below on the Roaring Brook Road, limped in without knocking. "Well, well. Ironing clothes and reciting poetry all at the same time, be you? Look out you don't scorch that shirt, young lady. My ma, she always used to say, 'You can't do two things to-once and do both o' them well.' Is your Pa ter home?"

"He's gone to Eastbrook to do some trading."

"If you don't mind, I'll just set down a minute and cool off." With a sigh of relief, he lowered himself into the chair the girl placed by the west window, took off his wide-brimmed straw hat, and mopped his forehead with a red bandana. "Almighty hot for the first of June. This weather's good for my sciatiky, but it's bad for the crops. The almanac says we're going to have a June drought, the very worst."

The heavy flatiron came down on the ironing board with a thud. "A drought. How can that feller that writes the almanac tell a whole year ahead of time what the weather's going to be?"

"Don't know how he does it, but by golly, he generally hits it right. Well, guess I'd better be going along."

"That old man just loves to croak," the girl said to herself, and went on reading—

"It droppeth as the gentle rain from heaven …

"The gentle rain from heaven," she repeated. Suppose the almanac was right about the drought. All at once she noticed how dry the earth was around the sweet peas under the kitchen window. She closed the book. It was impossible to keep her mind on Shakespeare now.

At noon, Nancy, the sorrel mare, came jog-trotting down the road bringing Mr. Bradley home from Eastbrook. The back of the box wagon was full of packages, crates, and boxes. "We're going to need those for sure," Janet thought exultingly on seeing the stacks of new berry baskets.

That evening, she noticed how her father stood in the yard and looked anxiously at the cloudless western sky. "You don't think we're going to have a drought, do you?"

"Well, we do need rain bad."

"Is it dry enough to hurt the strawberries and the potatoes?"

"They'll be all right if we get rain in a few days."

The watched-for rain did not come. Night after night, the sun went down like a red-orange ball floating in a clear blue sky. It was the hottest first week in June on record. To make matters worse, a breeze blew constantly, fanning the last drop of moisture out of the earth. Little eddies of dust scurried along the white road and powdered the pansy bed, the rose bushes, and the morning glories that climbed over the porch.

Janet took another trip to the upper lot. This time she could not fail to see the brown, dry tips on the half-ripe berries. The small ones had stopped growing and looked seedy. She bit one in two. "It's as full of seeds as a ragweed stalk," she thought.

As one hot day succeeded another, the lines in Mr. Bradley's forehead became deep grooves. He shouted angrily at Nancy as she dragged a cultivator over the dusty fields, and he yanked nervously on the lines.

Janet was silent as she worked in the kitchen.

Molly came home from school singing a new song she had learned. It began—

*"There's no dew left on the daisies and clover,
There's no rain left in heaven."*

"Stop singing that. Stop it," ordered Janet angrily, after she had heard for at least a half-dozen times that there was "no rain left in heaven."

Molly looked at her sister in wide-eyed amazement.

"What is the matter with me?" the older girl asked herself. For the last few days, she had been flaring up at Molly over the most trifling things.

On Saturday night, Mr. Bradley reported hopefully that it was "clouding up." Janet ran to the kitchen window. Yes, there was, there actually was, a low bank of clouds in the west. The baked-bean and brown-bread supper tasted better than anything she had eaten for days.

The moment the girl opened her eyes the next morning, she looked toward the small-paned east window in her chamber. It was a bright rectangle of sunlight.

That morning at church, the minister prayed for rain.

On Monday, the sky was cloudless. The sun continued to scorch and sear the fields for two days, without even a shower to interrupt its work. Suddenly, on Wednesday afternoon, ink-black clouds piled up on the horizon. A dull rumble of thunder sounded. It was music in Janet's ears as she rushed about putting down windows. Her father was smiling when he came on a run from the fields. "It's going to pour. It's going to pour," he cried out jubilantly.

The thunder turned from a rumble into a threatening growl, then began crashing on all sides. A wind roared in the woods. Clouds tore across the top of Laurel Hill. Dick crawled trembling under the barn.

"Listen, Papa," shouted Janet in the midst of the tumult. Rain was splattering on the woodshed roof.

Almost as soon as she spoke, the downpour dwindled to occasional drops. The thunder sounded farther and farther away. In five minutes, the sun was shining. "Jumping Jehoshaphat!" cried Mr. Bradley. "It hasn't even laid the dust."

On the following Sunday, the minister prayed again for rain and announced that the annual strawberry festival would not be held this year, owing to the shortage of berries. There would be an ice cream social instead.

The Bradleys did not need the new baskets and crates. They sat stacked up in the barn, white and unstained, just as they had come from the store—looking like a tombstone, it seemed to Janet. Two-thirds of the berries that loaded the strawberry vines turned into wizened nubs. The red raspberries were a complete failure. So were the early potatoes; all the green rosettes turned brown.

By the middle of June, the only cheerful member of the family was Molly. "No more school! No more school till September," she crowed.

"Perhaps no more school all next year for me," thought Janet.

Chapter II

A Buggy Ride

"Just look at those red wheels! And rubber tires!"

Janet stood in the yard stroking the chestnut nose of a frisky young horse and gazing in open-mouthed admiration at the shiny new buggy. "Good gracious! You've got a new harness, too—with some of those stylish russet reins. Do you mean to tell me that this buggy is yours? I bet you hired it from the Eastbrook livery stable."

The tall, blue-eyed boy standing beside her burst out laughing. "Of course it's mine. You couldn't hire so nice and shiny a rig as that. Father gave it to me. Fanny's my own, too. I took care of her from the time she was just a little, long-legged colt. Don't you remember what a job I had breaking her in the harness?" He slapped the young horse's glistening flank proudly. "Now, young lady, how would you like to be the first person to ride behind her except me? There's a vaudeville show over at Wolcott's Grove this evening, and I thought it would be fun to go and take a certain girl who is sixteen years old today."

Janet grinned. "Just as I was beginning to think you'd forgotten what day it was! Can't think of anything I'd rather do, but I'll have to ask Papa."

Mr. Bradley, who had been sitting on the back porch apparently absorbed by the pages of the *Eastbrook Weekly*

Gazette, was already striding across the yard, taking in with a practiced eye the slender legs, small hoofs, and high-held head of the colt. "You've got quite a turn-out there, Stephen. That is a nice bit of horseflesh. But I want to know if she's safe to drive. Seems to me she acts pretty skittish."

"Oh yes, sir, she's safe and as gentle as a cosseted lamb. I've been driving her by myself for a month."

"We-ell, I guess you can go, Janet, but don't be out late."

"No, Papa. I'll be ready in just a jiffy, Stephen," she called back as she fairly flew into the house.

"Glad I finished making up that cherry-colored chambray," she thought.

Molly, looking extremely sober, stopped in the midst of fashioning a full-skirted doll out of a hollyhock blossom and followed her sister into the house and upstairs. "If Steve Warren was polite, he'd ask me to go, too," she declared in a tone of offended dignity. The child could never understand why she should not do everything Janet did.

"You're too little to gad about nights," said her sister, stepping out of her everyday dress of dark blue percale and her everyday petticoats.

This was, of course, exactly the wrong answer to make to an old little girl like Molly. "Janet's got a beau! Janet's got a beau!" she proclaimed impishly in a voice loud enough to be heard in the yard below.

"If you say that once more, I'll never let you wear my cloverleaf brooch again or put my perfume on your handkerchiefs."

Molly looked at the four-leaf clover pin on the pincushion and the bottle of cheap perfume that stood on the bureau beside it. Quiet reigned instantly. Presently, she was offering to pull out some basting threads that had been overlooked in finishing the new dress.

When Janet came out on the porch, her hair, carefully dampened by steam from the teakettle, was curled in ringlets at her temples and around her ears. The thick dark braid, doubled up into a knob, was tied at her neck with a huge butterfly bow of black ribbon. Her cheeks glowed after a vigorous rubbing with a Turkish towel, and instead of the blue percale, she wore the new red chambray.

Stephen looked at her with unconcealed admiration. "I guess you'll do to ride in a red-wheeled buggy. My, but you look grown-up in that long dress," he added, looking down at the bottom of the hem of the full skirt that just cleared the girl's slender ankles.

Janet looked down too, a little self-consciously. It was the first ankle-length skirt she had ever worn.

Mr. Bradley kept tight hold of Fanny's bridle until the boy, having helped Janet into the buggy, had jumped in and gathered up the reins. The colt pawed impatiently at the ground.

"Now you drive carefully, young man. And, Janet, I shall expect you back by ten o'clock."

"Yes, Papa."

"Can't I go?" asked Molly wistfully.

"You can go way, way back and sit down," said Stephen teasingly over his shoulder as Fanny started out of the yard like a harnessed lightning bolt.

"Smarty, smarty, smarty!" shouted Molly to conceal her humiliation. "He thinks he's awful smart, don't he, Papa?"

The boy and girl in the buggy were in high spirits and as talkative as the owls that hooted back and forth across the wooded road.

"Rubber! Rubber! Rubberneck!" called Stephen cheerfully to the Matthews children when they came running out of the house to stare at the new rig.

"Can't Fanny go, though? I believe she's faster than the doctor's horse. Why, she could almost beat an automobile!" Janet was ecstatic.

"I'd be willing to race her with Black Bess, but I shan't try her with an auto. Fan would be so scared, she'd rear up and break the harness all to pieces, most likely. Did you know that some of those machines can go twenty-five miles an hour?"

The girl gasped. "It must feel like flying. Papa says autos won't ever take the place of horses. They break down too easily. Just rich men's playthings—that's what he calls them."

"My dad talks that way, too, but it wouldn't surprise me if we all were riding in them someday. Maybe horses will be just playthings by the time you and I are old."

Janet laughed as if the boy had made a ridiculous joke.

"Come on, Fan. Now show what *you* can do when you let yourself out." Stephen had only to jiggle the whip in its socket to persuade the horse to make her hoofs fairly fly over the level stretch across Sandy Plains. She trotted even faster when they turned onto the pine-woods-bordered road that led to Wolcott Pond and she smelled the horses tied in the grove.

"Listen," cried Janet, "the show's begun." Lively strains of music played on a tin-panny piano floated to meet them. "I do hope we haven't missed much. And just look at the water with the moonlight on it. Isn't this fun!" She was as excited as a child at a circus.

As soon as Fanny was tied to a hitching post, the two young people started on a run toward the brightly lighted outdoor stage under the tall pines, stopping only long enough for Stephen to buy two packages of Cracker Jacks and a roll of thin sugar wafers.

It was a night of nights for Janet. Excitement kindled her cheeks till they were as red as the painted face of the lady who peeped coyly from under a twirling parasol and sang, "In the Good Old Summertime." The glittering spangles on the tight-rope walker's satin skirt were no brighter than the dark eyes of the girl who watched breathlessly.

"Isn't it wonderful?" she said between bites of Cracker Jack during the intermission. "Almost like going to a real theater."

"Well, it's a pretty good show, but it's not much like going to the theater." The boy's tone was slightly toplofty. Earlier in the summer, on a visit to his uncle and aunt in Worcester, he had seen a second-rate company perform *Rip Van Winkle* and had been talking about it ever since.

"Anyway," went on Janet, whose enthusiasm could not be dampened, "it's lots more fun than Chautauqua." Up to this evening, the only vaudeville acts she had ever seen were the lighter numbers in Chautauqua programs at Hemlock Park.

Watching jugglers, magicians, cakewalkers, and trapeze artists, she lost all track of time, all sense of reality. The yellow-haired, coy soloist was a creature from another world. So was the handsome young man in a striped blazer who seemed to be looking right at her as he sang—

> *"Oh, promise me that some day you and I*
> *Will take our love together to some sky …"*

Even after the curtain had fallen and the footlights had been put out, she sat for a moment, unable to come back to Wolcott Grove, not hearing a word that the boy beside her was saying.

"What? What? Did you say it was a quarter to ten?" she asked suddenly, in complete amazement. "Oh, Papa will never let me go anywhere with you again."

"Don't you worry. Fanny and I will get you back by ten-fifteen. You've no idea how fast that colt can pick up the dust when she's headed for home."

Fanny lived up to her reputation, even trotting up the low hills. Reassured by the flight of miles under the red wheels, Janet relaxed and presently was singing "In the Good Old Summertime" in imitation of the golden-haired singer.

Stephen placed his arm along the back of the buggy seat, like a real beau, and hummed, "Oh, Promise Me!"

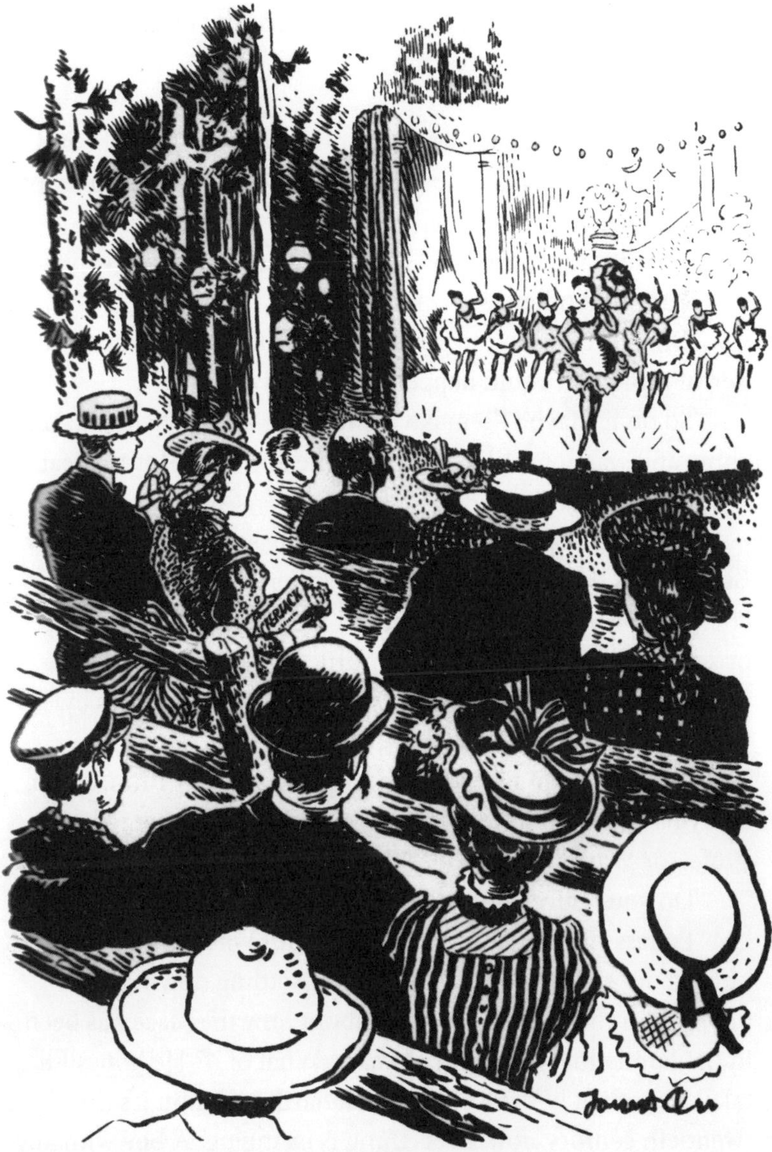

At the sound of the young people's happy voices, the whip-poor-wills ceased their plaintive songs and fled on noiseless wings into the woods.

"Do you know why Papa gave me this new buggy and harness?" asked Stephen presently.

"No. Why?"

"To make me want to stay at home and run the farm and the sawmill, but I shan't do it. I'm going to make something of myself. I'm going to college."

"You're going to *college*?" The girl's voice was filled with awe.

"Yup. To Amherst."

"Oh, Steve, I think to go to college would be the most wonderful thing that could happen to anybody."

"So do I. Maybe I'll make the football team. Then you can come and watch me play in a big game and cheer for the team. Wouldn't that be fun?"

"I should be proud as all get-out," she said enthusiastically. But she was thinking, "It'll be some other girl sitting there cheering—a college girl, probably. I'll be home washing dishes or scrubbing one of Molly's dirty little dresses, and he'll have forgotten me and all the other Glenbrook girls and boys by that time."

"Of course, I'm not going to college just for the fun. I shall study hard. I want to teach chemistry in a college someday. Professor Warren—how does that sound?"

"Do you really think you'll be *a college professor*?"

"I guess so." Stephen tried to make his voice sound casual but did not succeed. "Anyway, I'm not settling down on any old farm in the country. Pa talks about how the place has been in the family for two hundred years. What of it? He hopes I'll take over when he's too old to work hard. I tell him it's the twentieth century now. Everything is changing. A boy with any ambition just can't stick in Glenbrook. He's *got* to go to the city. But Pa can't seem to understand how a fellow like me feels."

"*I* understand," said the girl. How well she did understand the way Stephen felt!

The boy beside her went on dreaming out loud, but Janet heard no more of what he was saying. Her own unspoken words drowned out his talk. "Steve's right. A boy with any ambition can't stay in a place like Glenbrook. An ambitious girl can't either. In two or three years, all the bright young people of my age will be gone. Mary Clarke's going to Normal School in two years. Roy Miller has a job waiting for him in the Northbrook First National Bank. Delia Miller is going to Boston to study music at the Conservatory of Music. And now Steve!"

"Well, did you have a fine time?" asked Mr. Bradley when Stephen had said goodnight and driven out of the yard.

"Yes."

"How was the show?"

"The show?" For a moment, Janet had forgotten even the yellow-haired lady and the young man in the blazer. Somehow, it seemed a long time ago that the curtain had gone down in Wolcott's Grove.

"Didn't you go to the show?"

"Oh, yes—yes, we did. It was beautiful."

"Janet, if you're as sleepy as you sound, I guess you'd better go right to bed."

"Yes, I guess I will."

As a matter of fact, the girl was never more wide awake in her life. Yet it was a relief to go up to her room. She didn't feel like talking. Tomorrow she would tell Papa all about the show, even sing some of the songs for him. But tonight her thoughts were busy with more serious matters. Quite suddenly, on the way home, Janet had realized that she was growing up. Stephen, with his light hair brushed back in a pompadour, wearing white duck pants and driving his own rig, seemed like a young man. He would be seventeen in another month. And she, in an ankle-length dress, buggy-riding with this "young man" on her sixteenth birthday—why she was almost a young lady. Time didn't wait for a girl to say, "All right, I'm ready to grow up." Time did cruel things. It was going to leave her on Laurel Hill and carry away into a different life the boys and girls who had been her best friends. In two years, what would she and Steve have in common? "I can't go on much longer waiting, waiting for a chance to go to school," she whispered tearfully into her pillow. "I'll be too old. No farm and no little sister shall stand in my way. I'm going to make something of myself. But how, *how* am I to do it?"

Chapter III

Blackberries Are Cheap

The only berries that survived the drought were the blackberries. The bushes in the Bradley pasture were loaded down with fruit. For two days, muggy August days, Molly and Janet fought mosquitoes and red ants while they picked. Then they started out early in the morning for Eastbrook, with five milk pails full of dark, shiny berries stowed in the back of the wagon, carefully covered to keep out the dust. "Perhaps," figured the older girl, "we'll bring home five dollars. Then, next week, we'll pick some more. We might be able to make two or three trips before the berries are gone."

Before half of the four-mile ride was over, the sun was beating down with blistering heat. Janet could feel her shoulders burning under her thin shirtwaist. "It's going to be a scorcher," she prophesied disgustedly.

On the edge of the town, they began to take turns knocking at back doors and repeating the formula— "Want to buy some blackberries? They're big ones, and all picked over clean."

"Everybody says the same thing," reported Molly disgustedly at the end of her first hour of peddling. "They all just bought some yesterday." She had only sold two quarts. Janet lifted her stiff sailor hat and mopped the perspiration from her forehead. "I only sold three. One woman asked me, 'Where in the world do all you kids come from anyway?' She told me there were three different sets of boys along yesterday peddling blackberries."

At noon, only one of the five pails was empty. The two girls sat in the wagon under a tree and ate the contents of a dinner pail in silence. Janet looked down the elm-lined street to the modest high school building. In about six weeks, those rooms would be filled with boys and girls again. And she—unless a miracle happened—would not be one of them.

"We'll have to lower the price to eight cents a quart," she told Molly. "I guess blackberries are a drug on the market this year all right. And I thought we'd make a lot of money selling them."

When the town hall clock struck four, there were still two pails full of berries unsold. "How many quarts you got?" asked a shrewd-eyed woman, who did not fail to notice how hot and tired-looking the girl on her doorstep was.

"Twenty."

"I'll give you fifty cents for the lot. I can't use them now, but I might put them up for the winter, if you want to get rid of them."

"But that's only two and a half cents a quart," began Janet. Then she weakened. Her back ached. She felt a little dizzy from the heat. There was a four-mile ride ahead of her and supper to cook after that. "All right. I'll take it."

"Twenty-five, thirty-five, forty—" Back in the wagon, she counted the silver in the worn wallet. Three dollars for five dollars' worth of berries. Well, they sold them all anyway. Perhaps next week they would do better. Tucking the cotton dust robe around her legs and Molly's, she gathered up the reins and clucked to Nancy.

"Aren't we going to have any chocolate soda water?" The child's voice was almost a wail. After all this trudging to back doors in the heat, was she going to be cheated at the end of a trip to Eastbrook?

Her sister clicked the wallet open again, extracted a nickel, and laid it on Molly's moist palm.

"Aren't you coming, too?"

"I'm too hot to drink anything now," Janet lied. The truth was that she could not bear to spend even one more nickel of that precious, hard-earned silver.

***

"Let's play Make-ups," coaxed Molly that night after she and her sister were in bed.

"All right." Then, putting on what she considered a "society voice," Janet began, "What are you going to wear to Edith Fitzwilliam's ball tonight, Gwendolyn? Is Gerald escorting you, or is it Reginald?"

"Hello, Elaine," gushed the little girl. "I'm going to wear my pink satin. Gerald's taking me, and he has sent me the most beautiful bunch of pink roses. Don't you think I'll look chic?"

"You'll look just lovely. I'm wearing my new mauve chiffon with a bouquet of Percival's dark red roses and a red rose tucked in my coiffure." Janet was not at all sure what color "mawve," as she pronounced it, was, but she had read about a chiffon dress of that shade in the *Ladies' Home Journal*.

The game of Make-ups had been invented largely by Janet, with the aid of society columns and fashion notes in newspapers and of romantic novels borrowed from the public library. The two girls had begun playing it during those first lonely weeks last winter after their mother's death. In this dream world, they were young ladies of wealth and fashion—not Janet and Molly Bradley, but Elaine Stuyvesant and Gwendolyn Van Waters. Both had "golden hair and violet eyes," like their favorite storybook heroines. Arrayed in silks and satins and chiffons, they danced in mirror-walled ballrooms and sat on gold chairs while they were fanned and complimented by handsome Geralds, Reginalds, and Percivals. Again, dressed of course in the latest fashion, they rode tandem bicycles, cantered on thoroughbreds, or played tennis on green velvet lawns.

The elder girl was beginning to regard the game as childish, but tonight she was glad to forget reality again. To Molly, it was ever a delight. For her, Gwendolyn Van Waters was another and very real self.

The ball broke up at an early hour, owing to the sleepiness of Molly. By eight-thirty, she had danced her last dance. Yet, in dreams, she was still the fair, satin-gowned Gwendolyn, driving home from the ball in a coach and looking remarkably like a picture of Cinderella in one of Molly's books.

Janet too fell asleep quickly, only to dream of peddling berries. A woman offered her ten dollars for all she had. The girl ran to the buggy to fetch them, to find that every pail had disappeared.

Chapter IV

Mysterious Cousins

From the orchard where she was picking early apples, Janet heard the clang of the mailbox cover. That was always an exciting sound, and today it must mean a letter. This week's *Gazette* had already come, and the August *Farm Journal* wasn't due yet. She sped up the filling of her basket, then hurried to the house. Yes, there was a letter in the box. It was addressed to her father in an old-fashioned hand and was postmarked "Worcester." Now, who was writing him from there?

The minute Mr. Bradley came in from the fields to wash up for dinner, Janet handed him the letter. "Know anybody in Worcester?" she asked.

Her father shook his head. "Not a soul."

Janet and Molly waited impatiently while he hunted for his glasses, adjusted them to his nose, picked up a knife, and slowly slit open the envelope. "Well, I'll be hanged!" he exclaimed after reading the letter all through with maddening deliberation. "It's from my cousin Anna—Anna Bates. She and Dan have been visiting in Worcester and want to stop off here for a night on their way back to Redfield. Why, it must be at least twelve years since they were here before."

"I wasn't born then," remarked Molly in awed tones. It

always seemed odd to think of things that had happened before there was such a person as Molly.

"You were just a little tot, Janet. Do you remember them?" Janet didn't. "When will they get here?" she asked.

"They figure they'll be along in time for dinner tomorrow."

"Tomorrow?" The girl's voice rose into almost a squeal. "And there isn't a whole pie in the house, and only one loaf of bread. I'll have to bake this afternoon and clean the sitting room and make the spare-room bed, and—" She jumped up and began clearing the table without finishing the sentence.

Molly wiped the dishes as if moving about in a pleasant dream. "Do you suppose," she asked when the two girls were alone, "that the Bateses are like the Van Devanters?"

Janet laughed. In one of their games of Make-ups, the girls had invented these imaginary cousins who were as rich, as kind, and as powerful as fairy godparents. They came driving up Laurel Hill in a shiny Victoria drawn by prancing horses and whisked Molly and Janet away on wondrous trips to New York, to Newport, and to Saratoga Springs.

"Mercy, child! Are you crazy? You know we haven't any rich cousins, really."

"*How* do I know that?" the child persisted.

"Anyway, Cousin Dan is just a farmer like Papa and whoever heard of a rich farmer, except perhaps in a storybook?"

Molly did not bother to reply but went right on daydreaming happily about the mysterious cousins who had not been seen on Laurel Hill since before she was born. No urging was necessary to enlist her help in preparing for their arrival. Even the messy task of polishing best knives and forks with a slice of raw potato and wood ashes was gladly undertaken. She made up the big black walnut bed in the spare room with neatly tucked-in corners and fresh pillow shams, filled the blue and white pitcher on the washstand with water, and remembered, without being prompted, to put a cake of soap in the soap dish.

Janet baked pies and a cake. She gave the sitting room a vigorous cleaning, sweeping the worn carpet till the red roses were almost as bright as if they had grown and blossomed on the floor and wiping every speck of dust from the heavy, old-fashioned furniture. As she worked, the girl sang an old, old song she had heard her mother sing—

> *"Cousin Jedediah and Hezekiah and*
> *Azariah and Aunt Sophia*
> *All coming here to tea.*
> *Oh, won't we have a jolly time!*
> *Oh, won't we have a jolly time!*
> *Jerusha, put the kettle on,*
> *And we'll all take tea."*

Next morning, the girls were up with the robins. By eight o'clock, they had begun to steal quick glances out at the stretch of road between the house and the dip over the crest of the hill. Every time the clop-clop of hoofs or the crunching sound of wheels was heard, one or both of them ran to a window or door to look out.

Janet was almost as excited as her little sister. There was something about the arrival of these cousins, whom she couldn't remember, that stirred her imagination, even though she didn't let her imagination run away with her the way Molly had.

It was nearly twelve when a sedate black horse jogged heavy-footed up the hill. He was hitched to an old-fashioned phaeton that rattled with age. The two people in the seat bore no resemblance either to the Van Devanters or to the rather handsome, comfortable-looking couple Janet had visualized.

"It can't be them," said Molly firmly. "They look like—like dowdy old fogies."

Her sister did not speak for a moment. She just stared down the road.

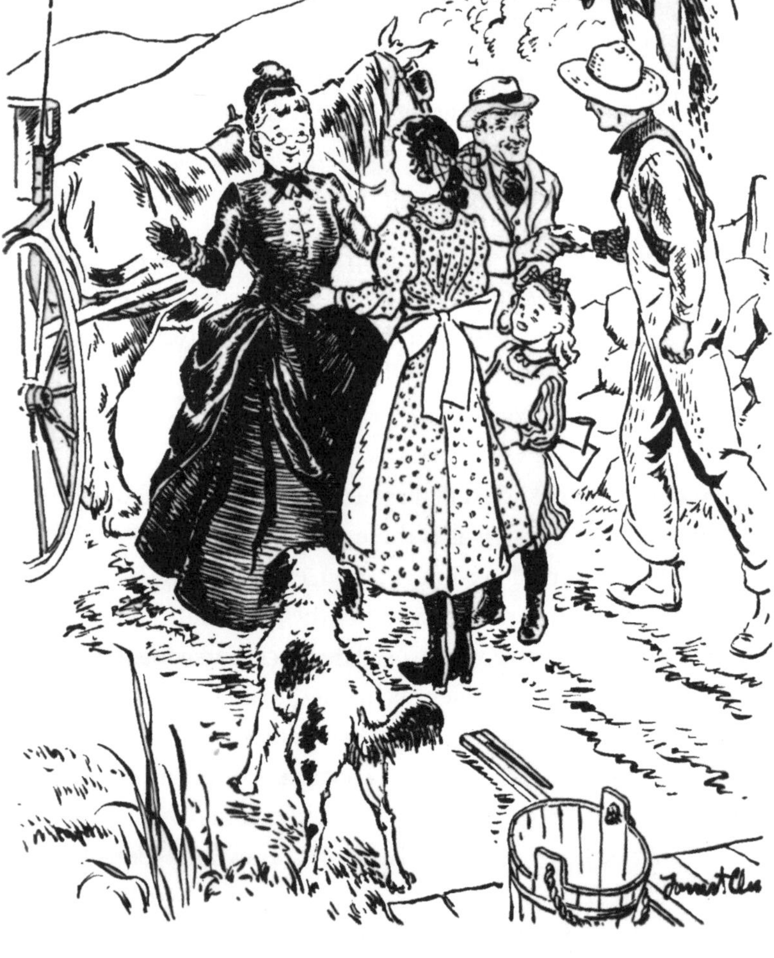

"They're turning into the yard," she announced tensely. Then, catching sight of her sister's face, she exclaimed, "Molly! Don't look that way. They may be plain and as odd as Dick's hatband, but they're our company and Papa's first cousins. Come along and smile at them and pretend you are glad to see them."

Hastily assuming fixedly pleasant expressions, the girls hurried out into the yard. The plump woman in old-fashioned clothes jumped out of the phaeton as lightly as a girl. Beaming upon Janet and Molly, she enfolded them both at the same time in a strong, warm embrace. At once, they found smiling no effort at all. In fact, like their cousin, they beamed. Cousin Dan shook hands with them, quite as if they were grown-up ladies, and this made them smile still more.

Chapter V

Janet Blows Off Steam

"What was it about these dowdy-looking cousins that made everything seem different?" Janet asked herself. It was as if they pulled contentment out of those worn leather satchels of theirs and scattered it about.

The whole family seemed conscious of this change. Molly was suddenly an angel child ready to do anything for anybody. Mr. Bradley relaxed and smoked his pipe in long, contented puffs, just as Cousin Dan did. Blackie, the kitten, rubbed against the guests' ankles and purred and purred. Dick, having left his favorite shady spot under the lilac bush, would not go back to it. His tail scarcely stopped wagging at all as he followed the newcomers about. Even the teakettle on the kitchen stove seemed to sing a merrier song when Anna Bates came into the kitchen, tied an apron around her large waist, and began to help Janet cook dinner.

"They don't act like company at all," Molly whispered delightedly to her sister. "It's almost as if 'she' were here."

Janet smiled. That was exactly what she had been thinking.

In the evening, it seemed to the little girl the most natural thing in the world to climb onto Cousin Anna's broad, white-aproned lap. "I wish," she said, "that you and Cousin Dan would stay here always."

"Can't you stay a week?" asked Mr. Bradley.

His cousin shook her head. "I'm afraid not as long as that, but perhaps we could stretch our visit a little. What do you think, Dan?"

"Well, I guess Charlotte and Tom can run things a few days longer without us."

"Our daughter, Charlotte, is just about your age, Janet," Anna Bates explained, "and Tom's thirteen."

So it was decided that the company that did not seem like company should stay till Friday, and Molly settled her head on Cousin Anna's shoulder with a deep sigh of contentment.

"Why is it," the little girl kept asking herself that week, "why is it that when you especially want time to go slowly, it always rushes?" Each of those days between Tuesday and Friday seemed to fly by as quickly as Christmas Day. They just tumbled over one another in their hurry to be gone. Janet felt the same way about this visit. She looked at the old clock and wished that, by stopping its hands, she could stop time. Even hours spent at hated tasks, like dishwashing and peeling potatoes, passed quickly with her cousin in the kitchen telling stories of her childhood on the Maine coast and singing "Blow the Man Down" as she made pies.

Thursday afternoon, while the others were on a trip to the Center, Janet and Cousin Anna took rocking chairs and sewing baskets out into the backyard under the wide-limbed apple tree. In that quiet place, Janet suddenly found herself talking as she hadn't talked to anyone since her mother's death.

It was almost as if another girl were speaking—a girl who had been shut up somewhere and not allowed to say anything. This other Janet told about the plans she had made for the fall and her bitter disappointment when these plans had been thwarted. She poured out resentment at her lot, envy of the young people who were going to school and would soon be leaving Glenbrook farms for work in towns and cities, despair of never having a chance to "make something of herself."

"I hate farms," she exploded. "I used to love every tree and stone on Laurel Hill. Now it seems like a place where a girl can drudge and drudge and get nowhere. It isn't fair for me to be tied down here at my age and grow up into an ignoramus."

"Fiddlesticks!" broke in the older woman. "You're no ignoramus. Don't you realize that there's a sight of difference between education and schooling—a sight of difference. It's fine to go to school, but when you can't go to school, there are other ways of getting an education. Why, sakes alive! Some of the greatest men and women that ever lived didn't have half as much schooling as you've had, Janet Bradley. Yet they were educated. They educated themselves by grabbing every opportunity and—"

"Opportunity! What opportunities are there on a farm like this?" asked the girl, not even conscious that she had interrupted her cousin in the middle of a sentence. "When I was Molly's age, I used to daydream about discovering suddenly that we had some kind of mines or oil or buried treasure on this place and getting rich—the way farmers do in books. Now I know things like that don't happen to real people—at least not on New England farms. The only Glenbrooker who ever found anything valuable is Billy Hastings. He struck gold, but he had to go clear to the Klondike, and he's never been home since, even to visit. Guess he's afraid coming back here would change his luck."

"You remind me of the way I felt five years ago. Dan had pneumonia that spring, and it took him all summer to get his strength back. I had to do all the planting and all the housework, except for a little help from the children."

Janet's face clouded. She didn't care to hear about her cousin's troubles or anybody else's. What she wanted today was a little motherly comfort and sympathy.

"As I look back on that summer, it seems to me that it was just one long backache," went on Cousin Anna serenely. "I began feeling sorry for myself, just the way you are. And I took my feelings out on the farm, just the way you do. Then one day, I discovered there was something valuable on that stony mountain land, and since then, things have been different for me."

Janet wasn't bored or disappointed now. "What did you find?"

"I found treasure."

At that moment, the rest of the family drove into the yard, and there was no more time for confidences.

Chapter VI

In the Good Old Summertime

"Jim," asked Mrs. Bates suddenly at the dinner table, "what would you say if tomorrow I tucked this oldest girl of yours into the phaeton and took her home with me for a week?"

"This oldest girl" drew in her breath with a little gasp and held it while she waited for her father to speak.

"Why—er—I guess we can manage without her. Molly's getting to be a mighty good little housekeeper, and I'm not such a bad cook myself."

Janet let out her breath. Her smile was like a candle lighted in a dark room.

"That's fine," said Cousin Anna. "We all get to the point once in a while when we need a change more than we need food or sleep or medicine, and that's the case with Janet right now. I believe she and Charlotte will have a real good time together."

Mr. Bradley looked across the table at his daughter and nodded in agreement. If the mere suggestion of a vacation could work such a transformation, what might not the visit itself accomplish?

Quite a different change had taken place in the face of his young daughter. She looked like a forlorn, orphaned owl.

At the sight of her quivering lip, the head of the family took prompt action.

"You and I, Molly, will have fun when we get your big sister out of the way. You just wait and see if we don't. The first day of next week, you'll pack up some lunch, and I'll hitch up Nancy, and we'll drive over to Mount Tom."

"Honest and truly, Papa?"

"Yes, honest and truly."

"Up in the cable car to the top?"

"Right up to the top."

Now both the girls were smiling.

***

"Cousin Anna," asked Janet as soon as the two were alone together, "what did you mean when you told me you'd found treasure on your place?"

"Just what I said, and when we get home, I'll show it to you."

That was all Anna Bates would tell her.

***

Janet leaned back on the wide buggy seat and sang softly to the accompaniment of Black Joe's hoof beats. Forgotten was the old house as soon as its dark shape had vanished behind the woods. Forgotten were the man and little girl who had stood on the porch waving goodbye. She was off on a two-day drive up into the Berkshire Hills, and she felt as carefree as a gypsy. What fun to be rolling along up one hill and down another, over rushing streams, through the cool, dark tunnels made by covered bridges! When had food ever tasted as good as did that picnic lunch eaten under a tree by the side of the road? At sunset, as the whip-poor-wills began to whistle, Cousin Dan drove into the dooryard of a village boarding house, and for the first time in her life, Janet was a "summer boarder." It made her feel leisurely and ladylike to sit on the long veranda in a rocking chair after supper and let somebody else wash the dishes.

On the second day, Black Joe had to slow down as the hills grew steeper and the valleys narrower. Then the girl began to hope that the fifty-mile trip might stretch out into a three-day drive. She would have loved one more night and one more day of being a summer boarder.

Yet, when late in the afternoon they came in sight of the Bateses' house, Janet was glad to be there. Homes, she had often thought, were like their owners. Certainly this one was like Cousin Anna—large, cheerful, comfortable. It shone with a coat of spotless white paint, seeming all the whiter against a background of dark pine woods. There was a wide, shady porch on one side, where a hammock swung in the breeze and rocking chairs with turkey-red cushions invited one to rest. The yard was blazing with scarlet cannas and scarlet geraniums and orange marigolds.

"What a beautiful place!"

"It's very like your house," said her cousin. "At least, it was till we put on the porch and painted it."

"Was it possible," Janet asked herself, "that the weathered old house on Laurel Hill needed only a new dress and a few trimmings to be as bright and cheerful as this one?"

Down the road a girl, a boy, and a collie dog came running to meet the travelers. The girl looked the way her mother might have looked twenty years ago. "She's just about my height, but not skinny like me. Her hair is straight, but it's a lovely color—almost as yellow as the center of a daisy—and her eyes are even bluer than Cousin Anna's. Or does that blue dress make them look bluer than they really are? She has the nicest smile I ever saw." Thus the dark girl in the buggy appraised the fair girl in the road.

Tom looked nice, too. She liked his grin. Of course, he was

just a kid to her. The three years between thirteen and sixteen make such a difference.

By the time Janet had been shown the half-grown puppies, had helped feed the calves, given the colt a lump of sugar, played a game of croquet with Charlotte and Tom, and eaten supper, she felt almost as much at home as if she had always lived there.

"Will I see that treasure tonight?" she asked when the family was all sitting together on the porch.

Cousin Anna shook her head. "It'll be dark in a few minutes now, but I'll show it to you right after breakfast tomorrow."

"Then you don't keep your treasure in the house?"

"Oh, no, it's in the pasture."

The girl looked across the road to the boulder-strewn clearing edged by pine woods. Could there be valuable mines of some sort in these mountains? Then she noticed that Cousin Dan was smiling quietly to himself. Was all this talk about treasure just a joke?

The chamber where Janet slept looked out to the notched top of the pine woods. Above the tallest tree, Jupiter hung like a great lantern swung at the top of a ship's mast. It seemed to be keeping watch over the place.

Chapter VII

Treasure in the Woods

Cousin Anna kept her promise. Next morning, as soon as breakfast was eaten, she started out with Janet and Charlotte and the dog through the gateway into the pasture and along a well-worn path.

"Why, I'd almost think I was in our woods at home," exclaimed Janet when they were walking on the brown-needle-carpeted floor of the pine woods. Red-berried partridge vine and trailing ground pine wove rugs of red and green, and clumps of fern and laurel bushes filled the open spaces.

"Yes," agreed the older woman, "I've been thinking that your farm and this one are a lot alike, except ours is a little rockier."

Janet peered eagerly through the trees for some sign of a mine or a cave. There was nothing to be seen but trees and bushes.

Suddenly Cousin Anna stopped and said, "Well, here's my treasure."

"Where?" asked Janet.

"All around you—the ferns and laurel and ground pine—green treasure."

So it was all a joke! The girl looked down quickly to hide the bitter disappointment in her face. What a fool she had been to be taken in by such silly, childish talk! She'd actually believed her cousin had a valuable mine or some old buried treasure.

"You see," Cousin Anna went on, smiling a little, for she had read the girl's thoughts, "we make laurel wreaths and ropes of laurel and wreaths of ground pine, pick bunches of ferns, and sell all these things to florists. It's grown into quite a paying business."

"You sell this stuff? For money? Could anybody—could I?" In her excitement, she stepped forward, slid on the damp moss, and landed with a great splash in the deepest pool in the brook.

***

Half an hour later, Janet, now in dry clothes, sat on the porch while her cousin told how in four years she had built up a large business in Christmas greens. As she listened, the girl tipped further and further forward in the rocking chair until it seemed as if she might at any moment pitch over onto her nose.

"Don't see any reason in the world why you shouldn't do the same thing," was Cousin Anna's answer to the question that had been interrupted by the tumble into the brook. "As a matter of fact, that's one reason why I wanted you to come home with me. You have a lot of this kind of treasure on your farm, too, and I thought you'd realize its value better if you saw what I'd done with mine. Now I'll show you my shop."

The talk was continued in the carriage house at one end of the barn, where the fragrance of last year's Christmas harvest still lingered. The old, crack-divided boards were covered with new tight sheathing. A new floor had been laid and two windows cut in the south wall. The space once filled by a buggy and a democrat wagon was now occupied by two long picnic tables made of rough boards and straight-backed kitchen chairs. In one corner stood a base-burner stove.

"This is my workshop. Dan fixed it up last fall. It was pretty lively here in October and November, I can tell you. We had a dozen women working in this room, and their tongues wagged as fast as their fingers did. They brought their lunches, and I made coffee for them at noon. It was kind of like a picnic or a church sociable."

"You hired all those people to work for you?" Janet was pretty amazed.

"Yes. I pay boys and girls to pick for me, too. It's a real business. Folks seem to buy more and more wreaths every Christmas. It's the style now to hang them on your front door and in the windows. And I keep getting bigger and bigger orders at other times in the year for laurel roping to trim up places for weddings and parties and so on, and for ferns. Of course, there are a good many expenses—cold storage for the stuff we make up ahead of time, freight, and so on. Still and all, we make more money from our green treasure than from any crop we plant."

In the eyes of the listening girl was the far-away look of a prospector who knows there is a gold mine and can hardly wait to stake his claim. She talked feverishly off and on the rest of the day about the business she would start on Laurel Hill. Even after she was in bed that night, she lay awake forming plans. Cousin Anna and Charlotte were going to teach her how to make wreaths and ropes of laurel. She would write letters to the florists offering to supply them with Christmas greens and sending samples of her work. Her cousin would give her their names and addresses. Of course, she couldn't hope to build up a big business in one season, but she'd start, and she'd make a tidy sum this year—perhaps even enough to hire Etta Hastings. The drowsier she became, the larger and larger grew her plans.

In her sleep Janet was at home—not in the house on the hillside, but up in the woods. She and her father were digging deep beneath the needles and leaf mold, and with every shovelful of dark earth, gleaming gold nuggets came rolling out upon the ground.

What a happy, carefree week that was! Janet was not a housekeeper, not mother to a difficult little sister. She was a sixteen-year-old girl having fun and being looked after and petted a bit by nice, motherly Cousin Anna. Her cheeks filled out. Gone was the tense, anxious look that had come into her face in the last few months. Every day, her dark eyes seemed to grow a little brighter, until, as Cousin Dan said, they shone like the buttons on her Sunday shoes.

Charlotte gave a party for her—a lawn party, with Japanese lanterns strung around the porch and across the yard, and ice cream and cake for refreshments. On foot and behind Old Black Joe, the two girls prowled about, visiting and picnicking and climbing the blue hills that encircled the Bateses' farm. The high point of the week was a straw ride to a nearby lake in the moonlight with about twenty other young people.

Or wasn't it the high point? On the train going home, Janet found herself thinking most often about the hours spent in the fragrant carriage house with Cousin Anna, learning to make beautiful green wreaths and long, firm ropes of green from laurel and ground pine.

She had thought it would be hard to go home. Yet, when the day came, she found herself begrudging the time the train took for stopping at all the little towns between Redfield and Glenbrook. She could hardly wait to tell Papa and Molly about her plans and to visit the woods and take stock of her own green treasure. One by one, the girl counted off the stations. Only three more stops before Glenbrook! Now two! Now one!

Familiar landmarks began to appear—the brickyard, the covered bridge over the river, the grist mill.

The train was slowing down. She flattened her nose against the windowpane. Yes, the little girl in a pink dress standing on the platform was Molly, and the tall, thin man was Papa.

"Gle-eenbroo-ook! Gle-enbroo-ook!" called the brakeman. "Don't be in such a hurry, young lady! Wait till the train stops."

Chapter VIII

Janet Gets a Letter

Janet's imagination played a strange trick on her that afternoon. She knew perfectly well that Nancy's sorrel nose was pointing toward the west and that a day was ending, not beginning. Yet, when the top of Laurel Hill rose beyond a bend in the road, it seemed as if the rosy sky above it was a sunrise instead of a sunset. Stranger yet, she could look straight at the weather-darkened house and see it shining and white like the Bateses' house.

"How bright her eyes are!" thought Mr. Bradley. "She's lost that droopy look, too. It's the same old Janet she used to be."

The first thing the girl did after changing into her everyday calico was to start out by herself through the fields. She hurried even up the last steep slope, for it would soon be dusky under the pines. Reaching the upper lot, she passed between two tree trunks that were like the posts of a wide doorway and was suddenly in a place of cool greenness and soft murmurings, her favorite spot on Laurel Hill. Throwing herself down on a bed of thick moss, she took a deep drink from the spring that bubbled up in the heart of the woods. Then began her tour of inspection.

Yes, she too had much green treasure. In many places the

ground was entirely covered over by trailing pine. There were stubby shoots of dwarf pine, too, quantities of Christmas ferns, and big clumps of laurel.

Along the top of the hill extended a stone wall that was fast tumbling to pieces. Janet climbed over it, went down through the woods on the other side, and presently came out into a long-unused pasture that was rapidly turning into a brush lot. Here, laurel grew in utter profusion.

"I guess I'll never run short of laurel, no matter how big a business I have, as long as this is mine for the picking," the girl thought with satisfaction.

Janet considered the other side of Laurel Hill as practically part of her father's farm. She and Molly came here for the first arbutus and for wintergreen berries and blueberries, and they waded in the piece of Roaring Brook that went tumbling over the lower slopes of this pasture. Yet the land was really part of another farm. Seven years ago, when the cottage under the hill burned down, the old couple living there had gone to stay with a married daughter. Since then, the place had been left to itself.

The sparkle Janet's eyes had acquired in Redfield did not wear off. Instead, it brightened as the days passed, especially when she laid plans for her business, and that was two-thirds of the time.

"Don't count your chickens before they're hatched," her cousin warned her. "You can't be sure of getting any orders, but I think you will."

No, she certainly wasn't going to do any mental arithmetic this time. She'd learned her lesson last June—counting strawberries before they were ripe. Yet each day she watched hopefully for the coming of the mail carrier.

"That Bradley girl's got a beau, or my name ain't Hiram Austen," he told his wife. "She's just as chipper as a blackbird, and she's always standing out there on the stoop waiting for me. Probably some feller she got chummy with while she was visiting up in the Berkshires."

"No love letter today," he called out to her, "just an ad from some flower-seed company, I guess."

A love letter could hardly have been snatched with any more haste than was that "ad." Janet held it in her hand for fully a minute before she could bring herself to tear open the envelope and find out whether Hawkins and Hatch of Boston wanted to buy her Christmas greens.

They didn't.

Neither did Reed Brothers of New York City, from whom a letter came the next day.

A little of the bright hopefulness went out of the girl's face after that second letter came. Suppose the other two florists weren't interested? What should she do? She wouldn't give up her plans. She'd get more addresses and write more letters and keep on trying and trying till every big florist within hundreds of miles had heard that Janet Bradley of Glenbrook had green treasure to sell.

There followed three days of almost unbearable suspense, made even more trying by the mail carrier. "I guess he's forgotten you," the old man teased her. "Cheer up! A girl as pretty as you don't have to worry about getting beaus."

"It's a business letter I'm expecting," she said with great dignity.

"You don't say!" He drove out of the yard shaking with laughter.

Janet stamped her foot in exasperation. "I suppose he thinks a girl couldn't possibly have a business of her own. Well, I'll show him that *I* can. At least, I will, if somebody will just give me an order."

The Glenbrook and Eastbrook schools opened on the day after Labor Day. Janet had dreaded this first day of school in which she would be taking no part. Yet, when it came, her spirits were never better. She packed Molly's dinner pail with good things to eat, feeling no regrets that she was not packing another pail for herself. Delia Miller and her brother Roy and Stephen Warren, driving by on their way to the seven-twenty train and high school, were greeted with smiles and a happy wave of her hand. After Christmas, she too would go back to school to start in where she had left off. To be sure, she would be a year behind Delia and Mary Clark and two years behind Roy and Stephen. What of it? Everybody knew that it wasn't because she was stupid.

There was a reason for Janet's optimism—a letter. It lay in a pigeonhole of the old-fashioned secretary in the sitting room. The creases in the paper were beginning to look fuzzy, so many times had it been folded, read, and folded again. Moore & Smollet of Boston wanted to buy wreaths and ropes of laurel, wreaths of ground pine, and bunches of ferns, and they wanted this green stuff in quantities that seemed to the girl enormous.

Ever since this letter came, a silly rhyme had sung itself over and over in Janet's head—

"Moore and Smollet
Moore and Smollet—
They are going
To fill my wallet."

Chapter IX

The Jersey Heifer

"I don't want to make you vain, but you're simply beautiful, and you have the loveliest brown eyes." These flattering remarks were addressed by Janet to a smoky-faced Jersey heifer. She and Molly stood in the barnyard looking on while their father brushed and curried the young cow's cream-colored sides to satin-like smoothness.

"There, I guess she'll do," said Mr. Bradley proudly. "Now, Janet, you climb up into the wagon and hold out this dish of cracked corn while I prod her from behind. And Molly, you hold Nancy by the head."

At first, the young cow balked at the preposterous idea of walking up two planks into the wagon, but the lure of the yellow corn shaken temptingly in a tin basin overcame her fears. In a few moments, she was tied securely into the box of the lumber wagon and shut in by its high board sides and backboard.

"Do you suppose Free'n'Equal will win a prize?" asked Molly as the two girls stood and watched the wagon disappear where the hill road seemed to dip into a bank of pink sunrise clouds.

"I don't see how she can help it."

"Honestly? A blue ribbon?"

"Well, anyway, she'll be the handsomest creature at the show, I know that," replied Janet, weakening her statement a little. It wouldn't do to get the child's hopes up too high.

This Jersey heifer had been the pet and pride of the two girls ever since their father bought her last year from a farmer in Eastbrook. "We'll have to take good care of her," he told them. "She's a little aristocrat—the daughter of a blue-ribbon winner at Northbrook Cattle Show." Molly had given her that long name. The child had come home from school repeating the phrase "free and equal" from her history lesson and had insisted on attaching it to the small calf.

Now, having grown up and having been put through a complete course of beauty treatments, the heifer was off for the cattle show to compete for a ribbon. Mr. Bradley would stay at the fairgrounds overnight to look after her. Then, on the morrow, which was a school holiday all over the county, the two girls were going to ride to Northbrook with the Warrens.

"Wish it was tomorrow instead of today," sighed Molly when she was starting for school. She had never been to a cattle show and could hardly contain herself for impatience to see the sights that awaited her on Northbrook Meadows.

Janet, who had seen the great show only once, and that four years ago, was just as excited as her younger sister. Yet, she could not wish this bright blue day over. Instead, she decided she would make it seem short by doing pleasant things. There would be no dinner to cook for Papa or Molly. She had already baked bread and pie for tomorrow's picnic lunch. The day was hers from now till suppertime. "Come on! Come on and dash about with me," barked Dick, who seemed to realize that his mistress was in a carefree mood.

"Come on yourself," she called gaily. She went cross-lots to the tall hickory trees in the pasture, scuffing through every patch of fallen leaves to make a great rustle. Having filled a basket with the white nuts that strewed the ground, she sprawled out on the sun-warmed red and yellow leaves, ate the sandwiches and pears she had brought along for lunch, and threw crumbs to the chickadees flying restlessly in and out of the bushes. The morning that had begun much earlier than usual seemed shorter than any half-day she could remember.

The afternoon hours went speeding by even faster, so busy was Janet. She carried her basket of nuts to the attic and spread them out on newspapers upon the floor to dry and ripen. Then she turned the layer cake she had baked the day before into a snowy mound of white icing and coconut, ready for the next day's picnic. After that, there was time only to wash her hair before Molly came hop-skipping into the yard, shouting, "No school tomorrow!" Then it was no time at all before Stephen put in his appearance, ready to do the neighborly act of driving home the cows and milking them. It took little urging to persuade him to stay to supper after Janet announced that she was baking biscuits and was going to have hot maple syrup with them.

Just as the big dripping pan full of golden-brown biscuits was emerging from the oven, the Clark girls arrived for supper and to keep the Bradley girls company overnight. The five young people had a merry evening, bursting into peals of laughter over nothing at all, playing tiddlywinks and Up-Jenkins around the sitting-room table.

There was no telling when Stephen would have started for home, and certainly no telling when Janet and Mary would have stopped talking and gone to sleep, had they not wanted Cattle Show Day to begin as early as possible.

"Ma said to tell you to be ready to start by seven," Stephen warned Janet as he took leave. "I'll be up about six to do the milking."

Janet set her alarm for five-thirty, but she needed no alarm to waken her the next morning. By quarter of five, she was wide awake, and at five, she was up looking anxiously through the dark windowpanes to see if the sky was clear. When she came downstairs, she found the two younger sisters, who had slept in Mr. Bradley's room trailing about in their nightdresses, too excited to stay in bed any longer.

Stephen was better than his word, arriving before six. Even then, the four girls had eaten breakfast.

"See you all at the show," Mary called back as she and Phoebe started home to change into their best dresses.

"I'll be there with bells on," sang out Stephen from the barn.

"Betcha a hundred dollars," began Phoebe, but Janet was already hurrying her sister into the house. There was too much to do for any more talk.

It was amazing how fast work was performed that morning in the Bradley home. A record was certainly set for dishwashing, and the big lunch basket seemed almost to fill itself with sandwiches and pie and cake. Even Molly's curls were less snarly and rebellious than usual, perhaps because the child stood perfectly still for once while her hair was being combed out, arranged in little curls around her head, and tied back above each ear with a small bow of ribbon.

Stephen milked the two cows with greater speed than they had probably ever been milked before, and he turned the crank of the cream separator so fast that Janet was worried lest he break that precious machine. Then he was off down the hill again on a run to "get on his glad rags."

The clock had scarcely more than finished seven strokes when the Warren span of bays trotted into the yard, hitched to the carryall that could hold under its black top Mr. and Mrs. Warren, Grandma Warren, Stephen, and the two girls and still have room for more passengers.

Janet and Molly were waiting on the porch, wearing Sunday dresses and Sunday hats. In a moment, they were off on the ten-mile drive, off for the Northbrook Cattle Show.

Chapter X

The Cattle Show

"Are we almost there, Janet?" Molly began to ask the question hopefully as soon as the bays were pulling the carryall up the long hill on the other side of Eastbrook. She kept on asking it every few minutes for the next six miles, then all of a sudden was silent, as silent as an owl in daytime. They had entered the city of Northbrook and were rolling along a macadam street past the City Hall—three times as big as the Glenbrook Town Hall—past churches of brick and stone that dwarfed the little white church at home, between rows of stores with delectable things displayed in their windows. Shiny-sided horses dashed past, hitched to even shinier carriages and smart yellow buckboards. A streetcar clang-clanged down the street. An electric brougham rolled by noiselessly. Molly was too busy looking to ask any more questions.

Presently, the wide street dwindled into a country road again, a road leading out to Northbrook Meadows. Before the tents and sheds, the race track, and the grandstand were to be seen, or even the flags and pennants flying from tent poles and ridgepoles, a strange medley of sound told the people in the carryall that they were near the fairgrounds. The cries of the barkers, the whinnying of horses, the lowing of cattle, the squawks of deflating toy balloons—these noises and many more were mingled to make one: the noise of a cattle show.

The bays put their ears forward and began to trot. The procession of wagons, buggies, and carriages grew longer. The white cloud of dust above it grew thicker and thicker. Dust settled in the folds of the linen lap robes. It dulled the brightness of the new red wings that trimmed Janet's last year's brown felt hat and powdered the long ribbon streamers on Molly's red sailor. It made Mr. Warren and Stephen, dressed in their Sunday suits, look like a pair of dusty millers.

The gate in the high board fence around the fairgrounds was the entrance to Wonderland. The Bradley girls felt as if they were walking into a dream. Along a colorful midway, booths offered almost everything the heart of a young person could desire—balloons in the shape of pigs that squealed and balloon babies that cried, toy whips, popcorn, peanuts, candy, lemonade, beautiful dolls to be won by tossing rings over their heads. A clown wandered about, grinning a grin that stretched almost the full width of his chalk-white face, calling "hello" to the children and bidding them come to his afternoon show at the tracks after the races. From the direction of the merry-go-round, cheerful tunes rose alluringly. Molly wanted to stop at every booth and to "ride on a wooden horse" right away, but Janet insisted that they find their father before they did anything else. So they turned their backs on the siren-like music and the persuasive calls of barkers and started in the direction from which plain, everyday barnyard sounds were coming.

"There he is!" cried Molly as they drew near the cattle sheds. "And there's Free'n'Equal!"

How strange to see their own heifer here among cattle from all over the county, chewing her cud as tranquilly as if she were in her own stall at home! "She's handsomer than any of the others, isn't she, Papa?" asked Janet a little anxiously.

"Well, there's some mighty fine cattle here, and some

beautiful Jerseys, but I tell you, Free'n'Equal's holding her own pretty well. She's making folks sit up and take notice."

"When will we know about the prizes?"

"Not till late this afternoon."

The girls wondered how they could wait so long as that, but a few minutes later, riding the merry-go-round, both of them had almost forgotten that their pet heifer existed.

"I didn't suppose the Cattle Show could be as much fun as the circus, but honest and truly, it is," pronounced Molly when the Warrens and the Bradleys were gathered in a sheltered spot behind the grandstand to eat their picnic lunches. Her usually solemn little face was all a-sparkle, like a dark tree alight with Christmas candles. Between bites of food, she hummed the wild sweet tunes to which she had galloped on a wooden steed. In her lap, she cradled an enormous rag doll won by her father at the pounding machine. How proud she had felt when her father brought the hammer down with a great blow that sent the ball shooting up clear to the top of the tower and rang the bell loudly. Lots of big, husky-looking men had tried to ring that bell and failed.

Janet listened anxiously to her father and Mr. Warren. "I thought she was a sure blue-ribbon winner till I saw how many other fine Jersey heifers there were here," said Mr. Bradley.

"Yes," agreed the other. "They're the pick of the county."

The morning had seemed exciting, but it was nothing compared to the afternoon. At two o'clock, a great balloon went sailing out across the meadow, and from it *a man leaped into the air*. It seemed as if neither of the girls breathed and neither shut her mouth until he was safely borne to earth again by that umbrella-like thing people called a parachute. After the balloon ascension came the races—sulky races, jockey races, and finally, to Molly's unspeakable delight, a race between Shetland ponies ridden by children. For her, this race was worth all the others. Never before had she seen shaggy little ponies like these, and never had she wanted to own anything quite so much.

Now the vaudeville show began on a stage in front of the grandstand. Here the clown turned cartwheels and tumbled about. Above it, a beautiful lady walked the tightrope, and graceful young people swung through the air, holding on by toes and teeth. Oh, never would she forget this day, not even when she was a grandmother, thought Molly.

"Come on," said Mr. Bradley, as soon as the show was over. "They'll be picking out the prize heifers any minute now." It was his turn to be excited. For this moment he had been feeding and grooming Free'n'Equal for weeks. For this moment he had come to the cattle show. His older daughter was hardly less eager to hear the awards. People turned to look at her flaming cheeks and bright eyes as she went running and skipping with Molly across the grounds toward the cattle pens. As for the younger girl, even while her feet skipped along beside Janet, her head kept turning around to get one more glimpse of the shaggy ponies.

"Oh! Look what they're doing to her. They'll scare her to death," cried out Janet disgustedly, pointing ahead. Three men stood around Free'n'Equal. One held her halter. A second had pried open her mouth, and the three of them were peering critically into the wide, pink opening.

The heifer took the examination far more coolly than did her master and mistresses, not even objecting when her small hoofs were picked up one by one. "As if anyone couldn't tell at a glance that she had beautiful feet!" thought Janet contemptuously. The girl teetered back and forth from her heels to her toes. She tugged at a loose button on her coat until it came off and twiddled the heads of the hatpins that held her hat on. Wouldn't the judges ever be done with all this folderol?

"It will be after dark before we get home," fumed Mr. Bradley. "Wish I'd asked one of the Matthews boys to drive home the cows." It seemed as if these three men were just trying to be slow and tantalizing.

Now they had narrowed down their choice of Jersey heifers to three, and Free'n'Equal was one of those three! Finally, it lay between the Bradley heifer and one other. The suspense was almost more than the family could bear.

"That other one isn't half as pretty as Free'n'Equal," muttered Janet to her father. "She can't win the prize, can she?"

"It isn't just prettiness that counts in a cow," he told her in a tense whisper.

"If I couldn't make up my mind any quicker than those fellows, I wouldn't try to judge cattle." This came from Stephen, who had joined the knot of neighbors and friends rallying to the support of the Bradley heifer.

Even as the boy spoke, one of the men attached a blue ribbon to Free'n'Equal's halter.

"Hurrah! Hurrah for Free'n'Equal!" yelled Stephen. Then he grabbed Janet and swung her around as if they were doing the Virginia Reel.

"Hurrah! Hurrah!" yelled Molly, in imitation of Stephen.

Mr. Bradley said not a word but stood looking at the heifer like a proud parent watching a child prodigy.

If the Bradleys had thought they could start for home as soon as the judging of the heifers was over, they were greatly mistaken. First, a man from the *Northbrook Times* wanted a picture of the prizewinner with Mr. Bradley holding her halter. When he discovered that Molly had given the heifer "that funny name," the little girl had to pose with her pet, too. Then farmers and cattle dealers crowded around Mr. Bradley, each trying to outbid the other.

"What will you take for her?"

"Name your price."

"I'm prepared to top any offer made to you."

Janet and Molly waited in agony. The idea of their father

ever selling their pet had never so much as entered their minds. Would he—could he—*do such a thing*?

"She's not for sale."

At these words, the two girls breathed again. Yet they were not quite free from anxiety until they were finally settled on the wide seat of the farm wagon with Free'n'Equal tied securely in the wagon behind them.

"I hate to leave the little ponies most of all," sighed Molly, looking regretfully back over her shoulder. "And next to the ponies, I hate to leave the merry-go-round."

Yet even now the danger of losing their heifer was not over. About a half hour after the family had left the fairgrounds, Joe Hayes overtook them; and bringing his pair of lively grays alongside the wagon, he hailed Mr. Bradley to stop. He owned the best house in Glenbrook and was First Selectman, and he prided himself on his herd of Jersey cows. It was quite evident from the covetous glances he cast toward the wagon that he wanted to add Free'n'Equal to that herd.

"Say," he called out, "that's a dandy little heifer—a jim-dandy."

"You betcha," said the dandy little heifer's owner.

"Was you thinking of selling her?"

"No."

"I suppose you would if you got a real good offer?"

"No."

"A mighty good offer?"

Molly glared at the First Selectman of Glenbrook. Both girls again waited in horrible suspense for their father to speak.

"No sirree, I wouldn't."

Glenbrook's First Selectman tried to conceal disappointment under an airy manner. "Well, if you should change your mind any time between now and spring, just let me know."

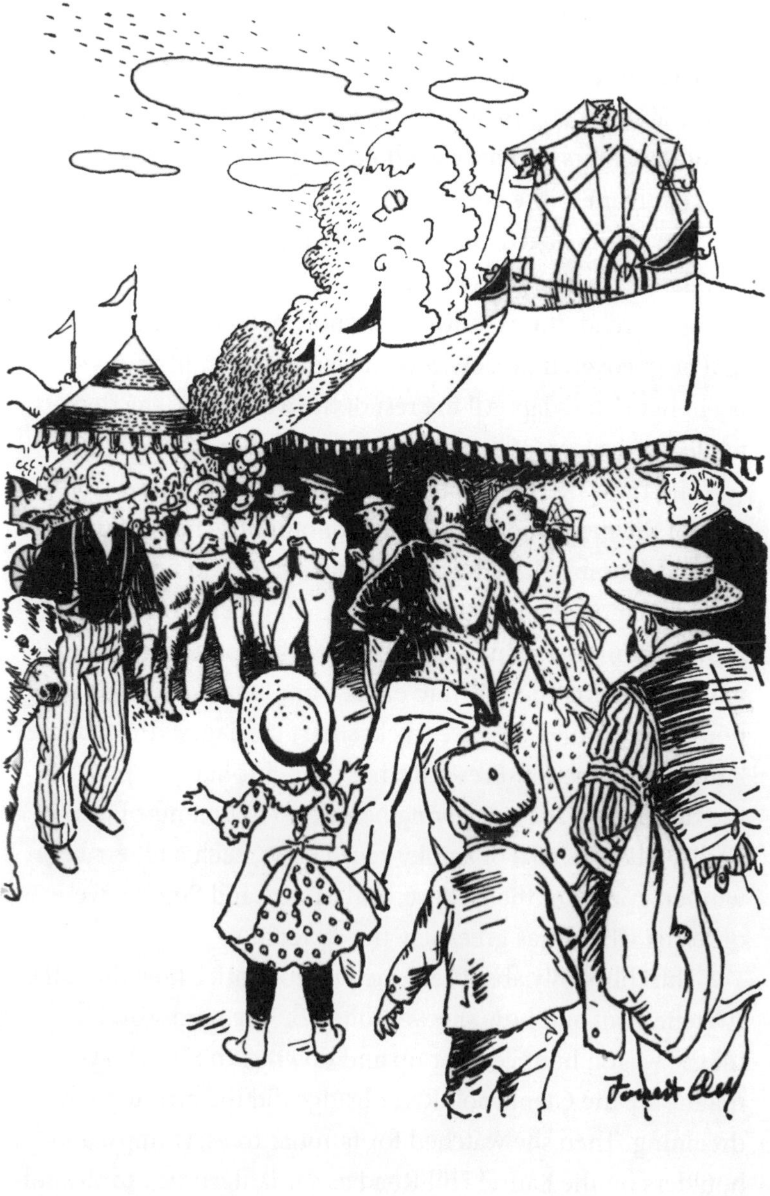

Whipping up his horses, he went dashing by, leaving a great cloud of dust behind him to settle on the Bradleys.

"You won't ever, ever, ever sell Free'n'Equal, will you, Papa?" asked Molly.

Her father shook his head emphatically. "You needn't worry about that. I'm going to keep her and her daughters and granddaughters and have a whole herd of Jersey cows and sell a lot of cream to the creamery."

The child relaxed instantly. A dreamy look came into her big, dark eyes. She was sitting on a little shaggy pony, cantering along the road. It was, however, a short pony ride. Before a mile had been covered by slow-footed Nancy, the child's curly head lay in her sister's lap. All the rest of the way home, she slept while the dusk crept down across the valley from the hills.

Janet was not the least bit sleepy. Neither the slow clop-clop of the mare's hoofs nor the monotonous chant of the roadside choir of katydids could make her head nod. That head was too full of pictures to nod. They went round and round within her mind like the merry-go-round—a balloon with a man floating down to earth from it; horses pounding, pounding around the race track; smart carriages; dressed-up ladies; automobiles. Presently, her thoughts had jumped into the future, and she was giving herself up to dreams of prosperity, where a herd of smoky-faced cows, each a blue-ribbon winner, grazed in the pasture, and Moore and Smollet were ordering Christmas greens by the carload.

Thus blissfully absorbed, she did not notice how the miles stretched out and how she was jolted on the hard seat. Not till the wagon bounced her up and down at the "thank-you-ma'am" by the Glenbrook River bridge did the girl stop daydreaming. Then she watched for familiar trees, stumps, and boulders on the Laurel Hill Road as the lantern tied to the tailboard of the wagon picked them out of the blackness ahead.

Dick received his family with hysterical yelps of joy. So rarely were they all away from sunrise till after dark, he had suffered agonies of fear lest they had deserted him. Barking saucily at Free'n'Equal, he hustled her out of the wagon and into her stall as if she were just an ordinary, foolish young cow instead of a blue-ribbon winner.

Chapter XI

"Keep Off"

The Laurel Hill squirrels stared suspiciously at the girl in the red tam o' shanter who seemed as busy as they were. Was she stealing their winter's food? No. She was just picking leaves, which seemed to them a silly thing to do. Every day now found Janet up on the hill under the pine trees filling sacks with sprays of glossy-leaved laurel and gathering bunches of Christmas ferns. She would work until her back ached from bending and her fingers were cramped from breaking stems. Yet always the girl hated to stop. This was not work to her. It was a kind of game carried on in the crisp fall air to the tune the pine needles played and the chickadees sang.

On Saturdays, Molly was a willing and capable assistant. The thought of the pennies she was earning kept the little girl at work even when Janet urged her to stop and play. There were so few coins now in the old pewter mug where she kept her savings. It still made her feel sad to think of the pink parasol she had planned to buy last summer with berry money. Probably she wouldn't make enough to buy it this fall either, but Papa should have a pink satin necktie for Christmas. Wouldn't he be surprised, and how handsome he would look in a pink tie! As for Janet, her present would be a ping-pong game like the one the Clarks had. Then—a copy of *Grimms' Fairy Tales.* The stories in *Andersen* she knew almost by heart, so many times had she read them.

One Saturday, when the two girls were in the woods together, they climbed the wall and wandered down the other side of the hill. Molly, growing tired of picking laurel, went off by herself toward the brook. In a few minutes, she came panting back to her sister. "Janet! Janet!" she called. "*What* do you think? Somebody's living down there."

"Living down where?"

"At the foot of the hill. They've built a shanty, and there's smoke coming out of a pipe in the roof, and a man's chopping wood. I saw him."

Janet lost no time in following her sister to a spot from which the new building could be seen. Yes, sure enough, a two-room shack had seemingly grown overnight beside the brook. A small load of wood had been fetched from somewhere. A cow was staked out, and a few chickens were running about.

"Sakes alive! Somebody *has* settled down on this old place. Who on earth can it be?"

"There's that man again," cried Molly.

"That man" must have either heard the child's voice, which was shrill with excitement, or glimpsed the spots of color made by the girls' red tams. He stood still and stared at the hillside.

"Do you think maybe we'd better go home?" suggested Molly. She spoke softly now.

"Why no, I guess not. Even if he has bought or rented the place, he couldn't possibly mind our picking this stuff. It's no use to anybody else."

Molly stayed close to her sister for a few minutes and kept looking over her shoulder toward the brow of the hill. Then, deciding that no one was coming after her, she was off again to fetch a last summer's bird nest from a clump of sumac below.

Janet, intent on filling as many sacks as possible with laurel before it was time to go home and cook supper, forgot about the new neighbor. All at once, a flock of crows came flying over, cawing indignantly. Their outcries startled her. "Hope that man won't drive all the crows off his place and onto ours," she thought.

Having filled two bags, she dragged them to the wall, threw them over the other side, and came down with another empty bag.

Crack! A shot sounded just below her. Someone was hunting right here in the pasture! Where was Molly? That coat of hers was so nearly the color of the frost-browned grass, a hunter wouldn't see her. "Molly! Where are you?" she called, running headlong down in the direction the shot had come from.

"Here I am," called a piping voice.

Oh! Thank heaven she was all right!

"Are you two young-uns trying to git killed?"

Both girls jumped.

The voice came from out of a thick, matted beard. Above the beard were narrow slits of eyes. The man was smiling—a kind of smile, it seemed to Janet, that a fox might bestow on a pullet he was about to grab from the hen roost.

For a minute both girls just stood and stared. Molly drew close to her sister and took hold of her hand like a small child.

"We—we didn't know anybody was living on this place," Janet explained.

"Well, somebody is, and that's me. I've bought it, too."

"We were just picking some laurel and ferns. You don't mind if we do that, do you?"

"Not if you ain't got no objection to dodging bullets. Like as not, me and my boy'll be hunting partridges here considerable."

As if to illustrate his remark, the man spat a quid of

tobacco out of his mouth, aiming at a round white stone and staining the center of it yellow. His smile expanded into a toothy grin.

Janet realized, and so did Molly, that what this new neighbor was saying with a smile amounted to a threat to shoot them if they trespassed on his land again.

While he spoke, the girls had been gradually backing uphill. Now, without another word, they turned and covered the ground between themselves and the dividing wall as quickly as they could without running. In her haste, Janet left her sack and a big bunch of ferns she had picked lying on the ground.

"He wasn't hunting partridges really. He came up there with his gun just to scare us. I know he did," whispered Molly, looking over her shoulder and not daring to speak out loud, even when she was on her own side of the wall.

The first thing they did when they were back in their dooryard was to go to the barn, where their father was husking corn, and give him a vivid account of the afternoon's adventure.

"Who is he? Has he really bought the Stanley place?" asked Janet when the story was told.

"He's Jack Libbey from way over Rattle Hill way. He's bought the place all right. Traded a piece of half-grown woodland for it. And he's going to live on it, and I'd just as soon have the Wild Man of Borneo for a neighbor, just exactly."

"Would he really shoot us?" asked Molly, her eyes big as saucers.

"No, of course not, but he has a boy who isn't quite bright, and there's no knowing what crazy thing he might do. As for Libbey himself, he's shiftless and mean, folks say—mean as a rattlesnake. Got mad at one of his neighbors and poisoned his dog. Wouldn't be surprised if he moved because folks made it so hot for him over there."

"He'd better not touch Dick," blazed Janet.

"The only thing for us to do is to keep off his land and not get mixed up with him."

"Keep off his land! I should say I would," promised Janet with feeling.

Not till she was in bed that night did the girl stop to think just how much the coming of Mr. Libbey might affect her. She could do without his old laurel this year, but if her business should grow, then she would need it. Somehow it had never occurred to her that she couldn't count as hers the green treasure on both sides of the hill.

Oh well! Why borrow trouble? It would be three years before she'd be through school and free to give full time to this business. By that time, this man would most likely have traded his farm for another. He was probably here today and gone tomorrow.

The next day, Janet kept on her own land. Yet even there, she received a reminder of her new neighbor. Nailed high to the trunk of a pine just over the wall was a large oblong of new pine wood. Painted on it in huge black letters were the words—

KEEP OFF

Chapter XII

Too Good to Be True

By mid-November, the Bradley place was astir with activity. Janet's father set up an air-tight stove in the "back chamber," which the girl had taken over for a workroom. Here, midst dusty trunks, old carpet bags, and boxes, her quick-moving fingers performed seeming miracles—making small steel hoops and lengths of hemp cord leaf out with glossy foliage. She worked longer and longer hours, stopping only to cook meals and do such housework as could not be postponed and often finishing a wreath by lamplight. Molly joined her here in out-of-school hours, making a game of piling fern fronds into flat, even bunches and wiring them together.

"I guess Thanksgiving dinner will taste awful good this year," the little girl remarked wistfully one night as she ate a supper of cornmeal mush and milk for the third time in one week.

Janet laughed. "It's lucky we're going to Grandma's. If we stayed at home, we might even have to eat mush and milk on Thanksgiving Day."

Now that the corn was picked, husked, and stored in the corn crib and the trees in the orchard were stripped of their red and yellow apples, Mr. Bradley gave much of his time to harvesting green treasure. When he was not in the woods picking, he was in the shed packing and nailing up wooden cases full of Christmas greens, or he was on his way to the depot with boxes and barrels.

During the last rush to fill orders before the middle of December, Etta Hastings came to do the housework for two weeks so that Janet could give full time to her business.

> *"By and by the harvest,*
> *And the labor ended,*
> *We shall come, rejoicing,*
> *Bringing in the sheaves."*

—Etta's voice rang out jubilantly as she cooked and washed dishes. And it was Etta also that wanted to know "what on earth folks bought that green stuff for, when they could just go out and pick it for themselves."

"Because," explained Janet, "when you live in a big city, there isn't any place where you can pick your own Christmas greens."

"Then why don't they hitch up a horse or climb onto a trolley car and go out to the country?"

When Janet explained the difficulties of getting to the country from a big city and of finding a place where one could feel free to pick anything, Etta decided that wouldn't seem like living. "Well, Etta," agreed Janet, "I hadn't thought of it before, but I don't believe I'd be happy where there weren't any woods like ours."

Early in December, a check came in the mail for Janet. "Forty-five and sixty-eight one-hundredths dollars!" She repeated the figures printed in red ink over and over. Could it be true? It was the first check she had ever held in her hands. And about as much more would be due by Christmas time.

Now there was no question about going to school after New Year's. With all the money she was earning, she could easily pay Etta three dollars a week from the beginning of January till the middle of June, buy her monthly commutation tickets, and even get the new shoes she and Molly both needed.

Down from the top of the closet shelf where they had been gathering dust came *Caesar's Gallic War, Beginner's French,* and *Plane Geometry.* That evening, Janet wrinkled her forehead as she reviewed the Helvetii, conjugated French verbs, and figured the length of the hypotenuse of an isosceles triangle. By studying hard every night, she would be ready to start in where she left off last year and hold her own with the best scholars in the class. How wonderful it would be to go to school again!

On the following Saturday, Janet passed through the pillared doorway of the Eastbrook Institute for Savings and handed her check to the polite young man behind the window. Her head was in the air when she walked out with a passbook bearing her name in her pocket and five crackling new dollar bills in her wallet. From the bank she went straight to Mason and Walker's dry goods store.

What fun to *buy* Christmas presents this year, instead of giving homemade gifts! Molly should have the "little pink parasol" she had talked about all last summer—at least if you could buy a parasol in December. Her father's gift was to be a pair of warm felt slippers; Grandpa's, some new ear muffs; and Grandma's, a handsome teapot to take the place of her old, cracked pot. For Cousin Anna, she would buy the most elegant handkerchief in the store—one of those with a wide lace border. And to herself—if her money held out—she was going to make a present of two of those silver bangles to wear jingling on your wrists, like the ones Mary wore.

On the drive home, the girl kept fingering the bankbook in her pocket and putting her hand down to see if the packages tucked under the seat cushion were safely concealed. She decided not to keep the bracelets till Christmas. She was going to wear them next Sunday to church. It had been a wonderful day!

Molly, who had been on a little shopping tour of her own, smiled to herself—a mysterious little smile. She had had to change her plans a little. Men, it seemed, never wore pink neckties. The one the helpful salesman had picked out seemed to her a little dull-colored, but it did have red spots in it. Ping-pong games proved too expensive, but she was sure Janet would like this new game called "Flinch." The girl in the store said everybody was playing it. It seemed a long time to Christmas, but a certain square package under the seat would be opened tonight, a package containing *Grimms' Fairy Tales*.

There remained for Janet another pleasant errand to do, now that her "chickens were hatched" and partly paid for. That was to engage Etta to take up again her duties as hired girl on the day after New Year's.

"I declare," said Etta's mother, "I'm real glad you're going back to school. I recollect how Miss Phelps, when she taught the Roaring Brook School and boarded here, always said you was as smart as a whip—the best scholar in the whole district."

The girl flushed with pleasure. It seemed too good to be true—she would really be back in school again within three weeks.

Chapter XIII

The Big Blow

In the second week of December, there was a sudden change in the weather. It had been one of those long, golden falls. Then the wind began to blow out of the east, and rain drove up the hillside day after day. Every morning, Mr. Bradley hitched up Nancy and took Molly to school, and every afternoon, he brought her home. On Sunday, for the first time in many months, none of the family went to church. Monday morning, ten minutes after Molly and her father had left for school, they came driving back into the yard. "The bridge over Roaring Brook is out," Mr. Bradley reported.

At sunset, the rain finally stopped. Then began the "big blow." All that evening, the wind roared through the great maple trees below the house. It was like the sound of a heavy sea. The farmhouse seemed to shiver on its broad, hand-hewn sills as great blasts of wind vented their fury against this broad obstacle in their path.

Janet, bent over her *Caesar* close to the kerosene lamp on the center table, did not notice for some time that the wind was turning into a gale. All at once, she was aware that her father had stopped reading and sat tense, listening. He got up quickly, put on his overcoat and cap, and went to the barn.

When he came back, he began stuffing the air-tight stove full of wood.

"Why, Papa," exclaimed Janet, "what are you building such a fire for? It's almost half-past nine. Aren't you going to bed?"

"No. Not while it's blowing like this, if I have to sit up all night."

"Papa's always nervous when the wind blows," she thought tranquilly. "I suppose it's because he got such a scare when he was a boy." She had often heard him tell of the gale that had lifted off the roof of his father's barn long ago in New Hampshire.

For a while after the girl climbed into bed beside her sleeping sister, she lay awake listening to the tumult outdoors. Twice she got up to push wedges deeper between rattling window frames and sashes. It startled her to see how wildly those great arms of the elm tree in the front yard were waving in the moonlight—just as if they were small branches. She hoped they wouldn't break off. What door was that, banging? Cuddling close to Molly for warmth, she pulled the comforter up over her ears to shut out the noise and finally lost all consciousness of the wind that tore at the windows and doors.

Sometime in the night, Janet woke suddenly. It seemed as if she had heard a great crash. Had the elm tree fallen onto the house? No, its arms were still waving. She must have dreamed that crash. Downstairs she could hear her father moving about. Perhaps it was time to get up. She struck a match and looked at the clock on the bureau. One o'clock. Why didn't he go to bed? What was the sense in sitting up and listening to the wind?

The next time she woke, it was six o'clock. Everything was still. It was hard to believe that a few hours before, a gale had been roaring through the trees. The first thing unusual Janet noticed, when she was dressed and downstairs, was that the fire her father had built in the kitchen stove was not burning well. Wisps of blue smoke curled around the edges of the stove lids. What was the matter with the wood? Then, in the buttery, she found to her surprise pans of new milk cooling. Why in the world hadn't her father used the cream separator? Had she forgotten to wash it yesterday? Was it out of order? She'd take a look and see.

The door into the back kitchen stuck. She pushed and pushed, then gave the thick boards a mighty kick. It gave not an inch. Lighting a lantern and throwing a coat around her shoulders, she went through the sitting room and opened the side door.

"Mercy! Mercy on us!" she cried out loud.

The long woodshed that joined the house and barn lay in ruins on the ground. The heavy wooden-pegged beams that had held up the roof for a hundred and fifty years had collapsed like tent poles, and the roof, flattened out on the ground, was for all the world like a crumpled tent. So this was what she had heard in the night—the crashing down of the shed. It was almost as easy to imagine the huge, moss-grown boulder below the woods rolling down the hill as the fall of this ancient, strongly built woodshed.

Raising the lantern, the girl swung it about to see better in the gray half-light of morning. She drew in her breath quickly. The side wall and part of the roof of the back kitchen had caved in where the beams of the shed had been battened against the house. Now she understood why the kitchen door wouldn't open.

Just then, Mr. Bradley came from the barn. His daughter had only to look at his eyes to know that he had been awake all night long.

Janet couldn't seem to cook breakfast. She moved back and forth between the buttery and the kitchen in a daze, bringing out things she didn't need and carrying them back again. She measured coffee into the coffee pot and set it on the stove without adding the water. Not till her father had finished

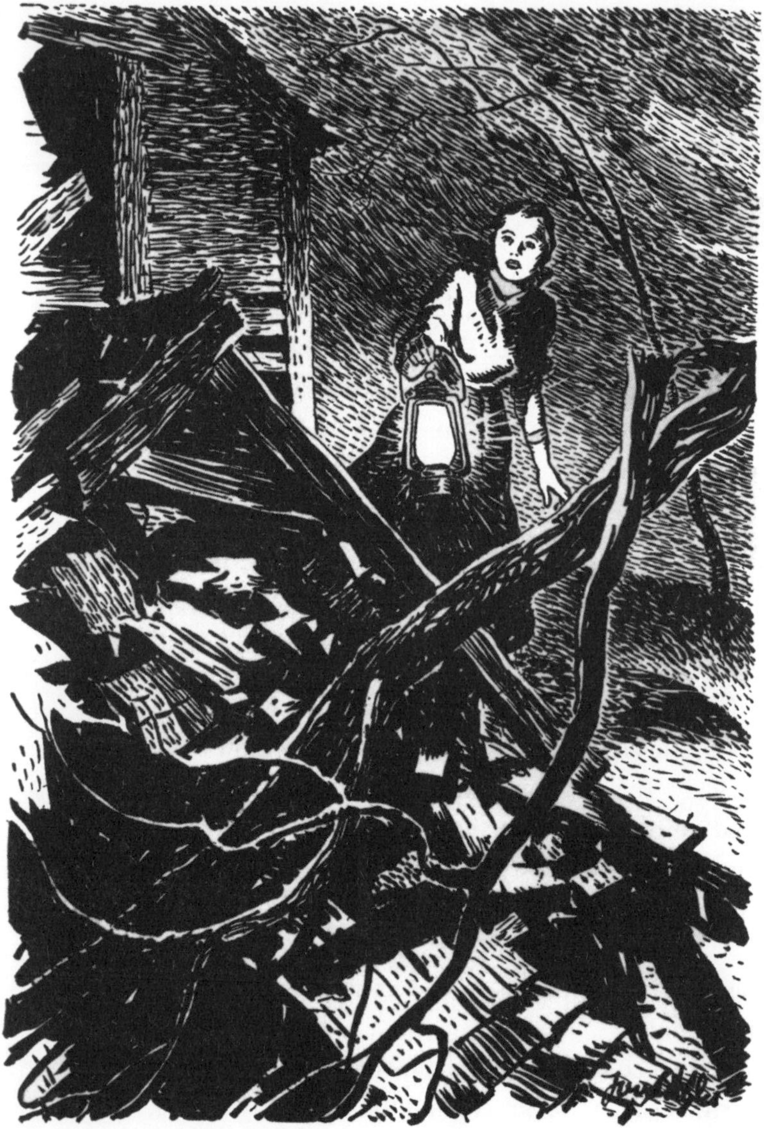

his chores at the barn and had begun to ask, "Isn't breakfast almost ready?" and Molly had called plaintively, "I'm hungry," did the girl rouse herself to quick action and try to enlist equally quick action from the smoking stove.

"Whatever ails this fire?" she demanded finally in tones of utter exasperation. "I've poked it and poked it and put in a lot of dry chips. Still it doesn't give any heat, and still it keeps smoking."

"I suppose it's the chimney," said her father.

"What's the matter with the chimney?"

"Didn't you see? The top's blown clear down to the roof."

Janet threw up her hands and ran out into the frosty air. It was daylight now. The ridgepole stood out plainly against the sky. Where the top of the wide central chimney had been was only a hole. How strangely altered the house looked—like a king whose crown had been knocked off his head!

Breakfast was finally cooked after a fashion and eaten. Then Janet wanted to know why her father had set the milk in pans.

"What else could I do with it without any separator?" he asked testily.

Even then it took her a minute to realize that the cream separator was probably smashed under the roof of the back kitchen. Thus, little by little, she learned what the winds had done while she slept. By evening she had counted up a long list of other articles that lay buried under the wreckage—all things in everyday use that must be replaced at once. The chimney would have to be repaired right away, too, and the roof of the back kitchen.

Molly, who at first had taken the aftermath of the gale lightly as a pleasantly exciting event, looked by afternoon as if all joy had gone out of her life. "Janet," she announced, "my sled was in the woodshed. It's prob-probably br-broken all to pieces." Sobs prevented her from saying more.

"Now look here, Molly, don't cry till you know whether or not the sled *is* broken. If it is, maybe Papa can mend it. If he can't, I promise that you shall have a new sled by Christmas, if not before." The little girl smiled right in the middle of a sob, then settled down quietly with her new book of fairy tales to read "Snow White."

It was not so simple a matter for the older girl to forget the catastrophe. She could make no sense at all out of *Julius Caesar*. Even when she took up the *Idylls of the King*, her mind kept wandering back from the "many-towered Camelot" to wind-ravaged Laurel Hill.

The night was as peaceful as the night before had been turbulent. Yet Janet, after sleeping soundly through the gale, stared into the dark night for hours. What a season this had been! A drought at the beginning of the summer had burned up the crops, and now a gale at the beginning of the winter had tried to tear down the house. Once again, a wave of resentment against the disappointments of life on a farm swept over the girl. When she closed her eyes, she could see her father's face, tense and anxious as it had been all day.

"Let's play Make-ups," she whispered to Molly, half-ashamed of her childishness, but the little girl had gone to sleep as soon as her head had nestled into the pillow. Her worries were ended with the promise of a new sled by her sister.

Chapter XIV

What the Wind Did

Early next morning, Mr. Bradley drove to the Center to see Ed Cowing, the local carpenter and mason. He came home with tales of widespread destruction. One of the stately elms in the square was down. The cupola had been blown off the Town Hall. The great maple in front of the Clark place was split in half. The huge limbs had just missed crashing into the corner of the house. Telephone wires were down all over town.

"John Clark says," he reported, "that he'll help me clear here if I'll give him a hand sawing up the maple, and Ed's going to start fixing the chimney and the roof tomorrow."

By mid-morning, he and his neighbor were at work transforming the wreckage into neat piles of timbers, clapboards, and shingles. One by one were uncovered the household articles that lay under the ruined shed. Every time Janet heard her father exclaim, "Mercy on us!" or "Great Scott!" she knew that he had brought to light something smashed or bent beyond repair. The two washtubs had fallen apart. The wash boiler was crumpled to uselessness. The wheelbarrow had lost its wheel, and the crosscut saw was ruined. Molly's sled would never carry her or any other child over the snowy hills again.

Mr. Bradley picked up the pieces and thrust them out of sight under a pile of shingles where the little girl would not see them.

The worst of all was the loss of the cream separator. Only the iron frame remained intact. All those wonderful parts in which the milk was whirled about—all were twisted and bent out of shape.

Tears came into Janet's eyes at the sight of the battered machine. A year ago last fall, her father had brought it home—a thing of shining paint and mirror-like tin. She remembered how she and mother and Molly had stood watching, round-eyed, as if Papa were a magician giving a performance. It had hardly seemed possible that milk could be skimmed just by turning a crank. There was some trick about it. Yet, sure enough, out through a spout came the yellow cream.

The tune that machine had hummed morning and night had been a cheerful sound in the house. At the first note, Dick and the cats would come on a run to stand waiting patiently for the warm, skimmed milk to be poured into their dishes.

"No more churning,
No more churning,
No more butter to make."

These were the words the separator seemed to sing. Now there would be churning and butter-making again until they could afford a new machine that hummed as it skimmed the milk.

Janet was strangely quiet all that day. Her thoughts were busy with examples in addition and subtraction—examples for which she could not find satisfactory answers. She counted the egg and cream money in the cracked blue pitcher, making small stacks of the silver pieces, then subtracted the cost of buying a barrel of flour and refilling the kerosene oil can. The remainder was almost nothing. Pulling out the secret drawer in the desk, she began to thumb over the dirty one- and two-dollar bills—money her father had saved from the sale of apples and late potatoes. "Twenty-five, twenty-six, twenty-seven—" she counted. "Thirty-five." That was only ten dollars more than enough to pay the interest on the mortgage that was due the first of January.

"There's your Christmas-greens money." A voice seemed to whisper the unwelcome suggestion in her ear. But they couldn't, *couldn't* use that. Anyway, Papa wouldn't take it if she offered it to him. He was just as anxious for her to finish high school as she was to go back. He'd manage somehow.

Next morning, the girl overheard a conversation not intended for her ears. She had gone down to the cellar to fill a pan from the Northern Spy apple barrel. Just outside the hatchway, her father and Ed Cowing were talking in low tones. "I may have to ask you to wait for your pay a little, Ed. Joe Hayes says he'll buy my prize heifer, and just as soon as he settles with me, I'll settle with you, but you know he's sometimes slow to pay, even if he does own the best farm in town."

"That's all right, Jim. I wouldn't ever hesitate to trust you."

Janet forgot all about the apples. Tiptoeing up the cellar stairs so that her father should not hear her, she went into the sitting room, sat down, and rocked furiously back and forth, back and forth, till the old-fashioned rocker creaked in protest.

Sell Free'n'Equal! Why, Papa would almost as soon sell his right hand. That meant giving up all those plans for a wonderful herd of Jerseys and a paying cream business. He mustn't do it. And yet, how else could enough money be raised quickly? The next few months were the leanest part of the year on a farm, with only cream and egg money coming in, and that always shrank in winter.

"Well, what are you going to do about it?" a voice inside her asked.

"I can't do a thing."

"Your help will probably never again be needed as much as it is now," the persistent voice went on.

"I'm not going to put off going to school any longer."

"How do you expect to be happy in school if everything is at sixes and sevens here at home? You can't be, Janet, and you know it."

Thus she argued back and forth with herself, rocking faster and faster.

Oh dear! Why did her happiness have to be all tied up this way with the rest of the family and with the farm? Last summer she thought she hated the farm. Now she realized how much she loved it.

As suddenly as Janet had sat down, she jumped up again. The chair went on rocking and creaking, as if too startled to return to its usual calm.

"You'll have to pretend for all you're worth," she told herself when she went down to the cellar again. "It will be the hardest play-acting you ever did in your life."

After dinner, making the excuse that she needed some salt codfish and some oatmeal at the store, Janet drove Nancy to the Center. Her first stop was at a comfortable place just outside the village. The house was large, wide-porched, and white. The barns were capacious and red.

"Joe's shelling corn in the barn. I'll call him," said Mrs. Hayes, trying to conceal her surprise and curiosity as to why this girl wanted to see her husband.

"Oh, don't bother. I'll find him." Janet started for the barn hastily, all unconscious in her excitement that she was being "bold" and "forward," as Mrs. Hayes put it to her daughter, Ethel.

"Could I speak to you a minute *very confidentially?*" she asked of the farmer. "It's a very private matter."

His jaw dropped at the sight of this girl invading his quarters and asking to talk over a private matter with him. "Why—er, yes. Certainly."

"It's about Free'n'Equal."

"About *who*?"

"That's her name. She's our heifer, our Jersey heifer that got the blue ribbon. You told my father you'd buy her."

"Why, yes, I'm buying the heifer. I'll come after her tomorrow."

"Please don't come. I mean, don't take Free'n'Equal. Just drive up tomorrow in the afternoon sometime and tell my father you've changed your mind. Will you?"

"You mean *he's* changed his mind?"

"No-o. Not yet, but he will after I've talked to him. You see, I have a plan. We can manage all right without selling her. I know we can. And it's very important that we keep her."

The man shelling corn grinned. "Pet of yours?"

She nodded. There was no need of telling Mr. Hayes all her reasons for wanting to keep the heifer.

"But what will your father think of my going back on my bargain?"

"It will be all right—really, it will. He'll be glad after he's heard my plan. But please don't tell him I've been talking to you. Keep it a secret just between us, will you?"

"Golly!" exclaimed the First Selectman to himself as he watched the girl get into the buggy and drive away. "I want that heifer. I've wanted her ever since I saw her at the Cattle Show. And now I let a slip of a girl talk me out of buying her! But what's a man to do, with that girl fixing her black eyes on him and pleading with him? She'd talk the ear off a donkey, she would."

Chapter XV

Acting a Difficult Part

In the quiet time of the evening, after Molly was in bed and asleep, Janet began to act a carefully planned and silently rehearsed part. Bringing out her schoolbooks, she laid them on the table, opened her *Caesar*, and began translating. Suddenly she slammed the covers of the book shut and announced that she hated *Caesar* and French and geometry, that she'd forgotten all she had learned, and that she didn't want to go back to school after all.

Her father looked at her as if she had suddenly taken leave of her senses. "What's come over you, child?"

She insisted that nothing had come over her and that she had been doing some hard thinking and had decided it was crazy to try to start in now where she had left off last year. She had forgotten so much; she would be the dunce of the class.

"You're just tired. Go to bed, and don't try to study anymore tonight. Everything will look different in the morning."

Janet followed his advice and went to bed. Anyway, she thought, he hadn't seen through her pretense so far.

In the morning, starting in where she had left off the night before, Janet went on acting the part of a girl who doesn't want to go to school. She used every argument she could think of for waiting until another year. A professional actress could hardly have been more convincing. Yet what hard work it was—to talk and act as if you felt a certain way when you didn't feel that way at all!

All during breakfast, her father tried to convince her that she merely "had cold feet over making the start." Fixing troubled dark eyes upon him, she insisted over and over that she "just couldn't go back in the middle of the year."

"You'll regret it terribly," he told her, "if you do any more postponing. The longer you wait, the harder it will be to go back."

Finally, he gave up arguing and said, "Well, you're old enough to decide this for yourself."

Once her decision was made, Janet found to her surprise that she had no regrets. A sense of peace took possession of her. Now she could watch Ed Cowing up on the roof slapping mortar upon bricks and laying them in their places without wondering when and how he was to be paid. She could skim the pans of milk serenely knowing that a new cream separator could be ordered at once. When she went to the barn to gather eggs, the sight of Free'n'Equal contentedly chewing her cud filled the girl with joy.

She looked into the heifer's soft brown eyes and whispered into one cream-colored ear, "You're going to stay here till you die of old age."

Meanwhile, Mr. Bradley, at work in the yard piling up boards and shingles, kept stopping to look down the road. "Funny," he murmured to himself, "that Joe Hayes doesn't come after that heifer."

Janet waited until dinner before she mentioned the bankbook in the pigeonhole. Then, in as casual a manner as if she were offering her father a cup of tea, she suggested that he borrow some of the Christmas-greens money to pay Ed Cowing and to buy a cream separator, new wash tubs, and a sled for Molly.

"We aren't going to spend your money," said Mr. Bradley flatly. "Anyway, we won't need it, if Joe Hayes keeps his word. I guess you'll feel pretty bad about this—I've sold him Free'n'Equal." It was perfectly evident that he was as unhappy over the transaction as his daughter could possibly be.

The girl began to talk fast. What was the sense in selling the heifer and letting her money just lie in the bank? And she'd be getting another check any day now. Why not go right down to the Center and tell Mr. Hayes he'd changed his mind? It was just a matter of borrowing from her for a few months. What harm was there in that?

"Well," he said, visibly weakening, "I could pay it back by spring anyway, when I sell those chestnut trees I cut for railroad ties. And Joe can't hold me to my bargain as long as he didn't pay anything down."

"Why don't you hitch up Nancy right away and go and see him?" she urged, not daring to give him a chance to change his mind.

Before Mr. Bradley had backed the sorrel mare into the shafts of the buggy, Mr. Hayes drove into the yard. Janet opened the door a crack and eavesdropped. A merry twinkle came into her eyes as she listened to the conversation between the two men.

"It's the funniest thing," her father told her later, "but Joe has changed his mind, too." The girl turned her face away. She was sure she looked just the way Blackie did when he had been stealing cream.

"Those lines are gone out of his face, just as if someone had taken a flatiron and pressed his forehead and cheeks," she thought that evening when they sat around the sitting-room table. "And he doesn't keep walking and walking around the way he's been doing since the gale."

By the time the old clock wheezed out nine strokes, everyone in the house was sound asleep.

On her way to school next morning, Molly carried a note to Etta Hastings breaking the news that the Bradleys would not be needing her services after all. Janet hadn't been able to bring herself to deliver that message. She had no regrets about her decision, but there are times when one doesn't want sympathy, and this was one of them. And she didn't want to see the disappointment there would be in the girl's face and in her mother's when they learned that Etta was not going to have steady work this winter.

When the first snowfall folded a blanket over Laurel Hill, only the piles of old lumber in the yard, a patch of bright new clapboards and another of new shingles on one corner of the house, and a top of new bricks on the chimney told of the havoc wrought by the "big blow." A roughly built lean-to sheltered the winter's supply of firewood. In the back kitchen, a new cream separator hummed its cheerful tune night and morning.

Free'n'Equal, all unaware of her narrow escape from leaving the home of her calfhood, stood and munched hay in her stall. Over the snowy hills, a small figure coasted on a new red sled. "It goes faster than the old one," Molly told her sister, "and it's so beeyootiful."

Chapter XVI

Christmas on Laurel Hill

"Do you think Christmas will seem like Christmas this year, Janet, really and truly?" The small, big-eyed face was pathetically anxious.

The older girl stopped in the midst of cutting up two chickens. Had the child read her own thoughts? She had been going through all the usual motions getting ready for the holiday, and yet she felt no enthusiasm at all. It was going to seem so different this year, whatever she did. Molly's grave, questioning face made her realize quite suddenly that making motions wasn't enough.

"You've got to laugh and sing and pretend Christmas can be a lot of fun, even without Mama to help make the fun," she told herself firmly. She had done a good piece of acting a week ago. What had been done once could be done again.

With a heartiness that surprised even herself, Janet exclaimed out loud, "I should say it seemed like Christmas already. Wait till you taste my chicken pie tomorrow. And just go into the sitting room and see the size of the tree Papa cut this morning. I believe it's the biggest Christmas tree we ever had.

"Bet a hundred dollars you can't guess what I bought for you in Eastbrook," she went on, when Molly had gone on a run to see the tree and had come back looking much more the way a child should on the day before Christmas.

Having fired ten guesses in quick succession, her little sister gave up. "Bet a million dollars you can't guess what I bought for you," she crowed.

A few minutes later, when Mr. Bradley came into the house, he found his two daughters singing—

> *"Dashing through the snow*
> *In a one-horse open sleigh;*
> *O'er the fields we go,*
> *Laughing all the way."*

From the biggest kettle in the house issued the mouth-watering smell of boiling chicken. Cranberry sauce bubbled in another kettle, and from the oven came the mingled fragrance of cornmeal, molasses, milk, and spice that would bake all day and be transformed into an "Indian pudding."

The pleased look that suddenly transformed her father's face was not lost on Janet. A little later, he started for the Center "to get some things he'd forgotten about." The contents of the bags he brought home caused his younger daughter to hop up and down and shout, "Goody! Goody! Goody!" There were English walnuts, a bunch of Malaga grapes, and oranges as big as four fists the size of hers.

"I guess the best part of Christmas is the night before," Molly wisely observed that evening. She sat in the kitchen with a threaded darning needle in her hand, making popcorn garlands for the tree, listening to the pop-pop-pop that issued from the corn popper Mr. Bradley shook over the stove, and sniffing the boiling molasses her sister stirred every now and then with a wooden spoon.

When the bread pan was filled to the brim with snowy flakes, Janet poured the thick syrup over them and stirred vigorously till every flake was coated with amber. Then she and Molly buttered their hands, shaped the sticky mass into balls, and piled them on a platter.

Presently, all three of them began to transform the hemlock that waited in the sitting room into a tree of many-fruited beauty. All the decorations were homemade, from the gilt star, with somewhat irregular edges at the top, to the snowbank of cotton batting around the bottom of the trunk. Besides the ropes of popcorn and the corn balls, there were streamers of gilt paper, balls made from bright-colored yarn, and red Northern Spy apples brought from the cellar and polished till they gleamed in the lamplight. The last step—tying on the gifts and tucking them beneath the branches—was attended with much secrecy. "Don't look now," one would say. Then the other two had to turn their backs. When finally the hemlock was ready for its great moment on the morrow, no one could go near it again that night.

The first up next morning was Molly, padding downstairs in woolen slippers and flannelette nightgown and trailing behind her the bed blanket she had wrapped around her shoulders. Her breath was like puffs of smoke in the cold air. The window panes were so thick with frost that no glimpse of the cold white world outside could be seen through them. She shivered, and her toes and fingers seemed to be turning to ice. Yet she would not go back to bed until she had made sure that her shouts of "Merry Christmas" had woken her father. Then she opened the outside door to let in the dog and the cat who whined and mewed on the porch after a night spent in the barn. A blast of bone-chilling air followed her as she scampered upstairs with Blackie in her arms. Even the pleasant warmth of the bed and the purring contentment of the cat could not keep her quiet long. As soon as the snappings and cracklings from below told that a fire was burning in the sitting-room stove, she grabbed up her clothes and ran downstairs to dress.

The clouds in the east and the snowy fields beneath them were just turning pink when the Bradley family sat down to breakfast, and before the glow had faded, they were gathered around the tree, opening the mysterious packages it held.

"How *did* you know I wanted it so much?" asked Janet when an oblong package marked with her name proved to be a copy of *Tennyson's Poems*. "It's got 'The Idylls of the King' and 'The Lady of Shalott' and all my favorites."

"I'm not deaf, and I've still a fairly good memory," was her father's reply. "Last Christmas you said you'd hinted to Grandma that you wanted *Tennyson's Poems*. Then Grandma went and gave you *Pilgrim's Progress*. So you have your wish, just a year late."

Molly hovered anxiously in front of her. "Aren't you going to open your other presents? There's one, and there's another." She pointed to two small packages evidently wrapped and tied by her own inexperienced fingers. In one was the game of "Flinch." The other, when opened, revealed a lamp mat crocheted from bits of many-colored yarn. It had a strong inclination to curl up around the edges like a saucer. The maker explained that it would stay flat if you pressed it down hard on the table.

The child was almost delirious at the sight of the pink parasol. Opening it and tilting it over one shoulder, she jumped up and down in front of the looking glass till the old floorboards creaked. "Look how pink it makes my cheeks," she cried. The china pig with a slit in its back, her father's gift, was received with a cry of delight, and when she discovered a small envelope containing fifty golden new pennies, her joy was a pleasure to see. One by one, she slipped them into the bank, shaking the pig each time to hear the chink, chink of her growing wealth.

Mr. Bradley liked his necktie "even better than the pink one" he assured her and pronounced Janet's gift of slippers the handsomest and most comfortable he had ever owned.

Now the girls began listening for sleigh bells and running to the south window. They knew from past holidays that it would be at least mid-morning before Starface had made the ten-mile trip from the Williams farm. Yet they couldn't keep from watching the road. It was exactly ten-thirty when a bay horse with a star on her forehead trotted into the yard hitched to a cutter. In the sleigh were two figures so bundled up that only their eyes and the tips of their noses could be seen.

"I feel like one of those Egyptian mummies they have in the Northbrook Athenaeum," Grandma remarked. She stood by the sitting-room stove taking off layer after layer of clothing—first her mittens, then the woolen tippet tied over her bonnet and the thick woolen shawl that was pinned across her chest. Finally, she emerged from her long, heavily interlined black coat and was transformed from a big black bundle into a slim cricket of an old lady.

In a few minutes, Grandpa and Mr. Bradley were heard on the porch stomping to knock the snow off their boots. They were loaded with parcels, boxes, hampers, and Grandma's soapstone that was put at once on the stove to heat for a foot warmer on the home trip. Now came the most exciting moment of the visit—at least for the two girls—the opening of the presents from Grandma and Grandpa. The three parcels contained dark red cashmere for a dress for Janet, a bright plaid material for Molly, and a horseshoe stick pin for Mr. Bradley to wear in his necktie.

Janet's eyes sparkled as she draped a length of the material over one shoulder and looked at herself in the glass. "It's my favorite shade of red," she told Grandma.

"Mine's the prettiest," insisted Molly, proceeding to trip herself up in the folds of the plaid.

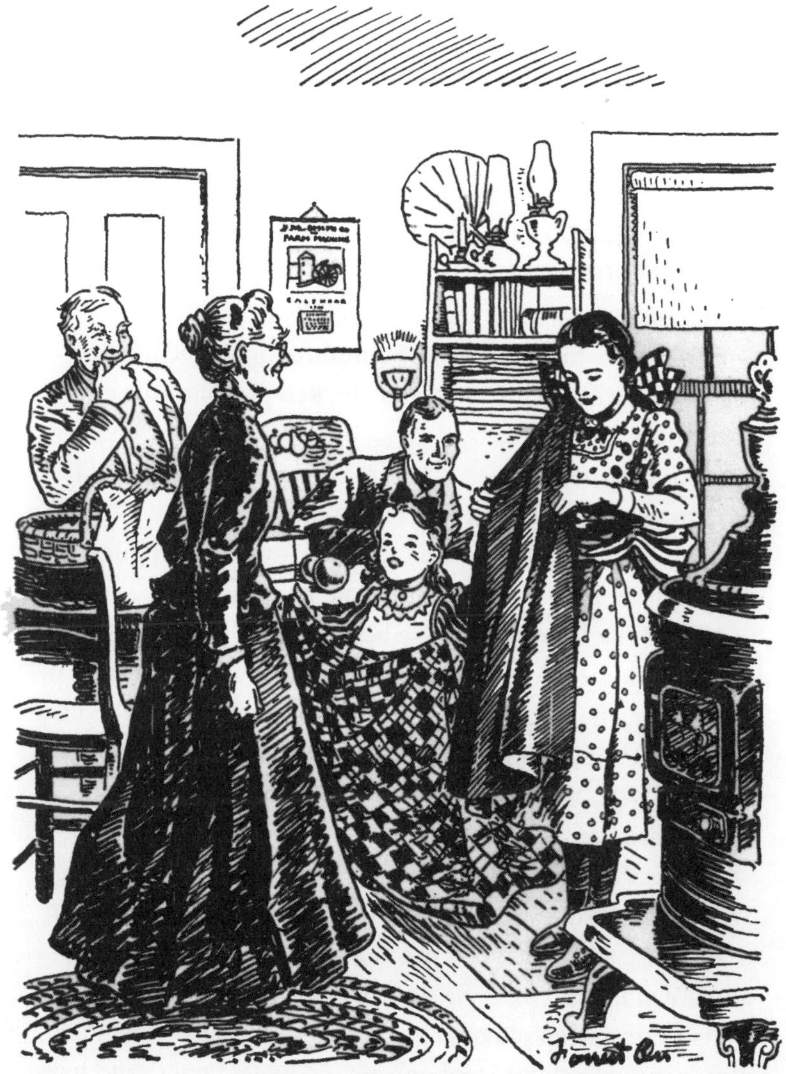

"After dinner, we'll cut them out and baste them up; then I'll take them home to finish," the old lady planned energetically. "Now, Janet, you and I had better see to things in the kitchen. We'd ought to get those pies I brought right into the oven thawing out. They must be frozen stiff."

Within an hour, the sitting-room table had been stretched to nearly twice its usual length, covered with the best tablecloth, set with company dishes and silver, and loaded with food till it seemed as if its sturdy legs would collapse. Finally, the huge golden-brown chicken pie was borne in and set down in front of Mr. Bradley.

Grandpa, a man of few and carefully chosen words, declared as he finished the last mouthful of his second helping, "I never in my life ate better chicken pie than that one, not even yours, Abby."

"Nor I either," agreed Grandma generously. "I guess I'll have to take some lessons of you, Janet."

Late that afternoon, when the old lady was wrapping herself up in preparation for the cold drive home, she confided to Janet, "You know, child, I've been dreading today. I wanted to stay at home and not be reminded of other Christmases in this house when Caroline was here. But I says to myself, 'I'll go for the sake of Jim and the children.' Well, I've had such a good time, I haven't thought once since I've been here about those other Christmases."

Scarcely had the cutter disappeared into the woods when Stephen arrived, calling "Merry Christmas" and announcing that the coasting was "just prime." He and Roy had been up and down the hill on their sled, packing the snow and pouring water on the steep pitches to make them slippery. Now they were going to get out Stephen's new "double-ripper" and have some fun. "Come on, Janet, hurry. Roy's gone back home for Delia. They'll be along in two shakes of a lamb's tail. Mary and Ned are coming, too."

Mr. Bradley couldn't see why anybody wanted to go coasting or anywhere else. "It's cold enough to freeze the ears off a dog," he warned them. "Wouldn't wonder if it went below zero before morning."

"We'll keep warm walking up the hill, and Ma's making a big kettle of hot cocoa for us," Stephen told him.

For once, Molly did not tease to join in her sister's fun. She had been out riding the crusted drifts on her own Red Rover and was sleepily content to curl up on the end of the sofa nearest the stove and read fairy tales.

Soon shouts and laughter were ringing out on the long hill. Under the weight of six young people, the double-ripper fairly flew. With each trip the road grew harder, the sled glided faster, and the girls squealed louder at the curves and bumps. There were spills, some intentional and some accidental. Twice, Roy, who sat on the end and pushed off while Stephen steered, was left behind sprawling in the snow.

Not till their legs ached so hard they could not climb the hill once more and fingers and toes were numb with the cold were they ready to seek the warmth and the refreshments waiting in the Warren kitchen. Then they pulled up chairs around the cheerful fire in the big cookstove and swallowed cupful after cupful of cocoa and ate as much cold chicken and bread and cake as if none of them had consumed an enormous dinner a few hours before. They said the same thing they said every Christmas night—that the leftovers tasted even better than dinner had tasted. As for the hot drink, it seemed to run right down into cold fingers and toes.

Janet and Stephen walked home together under diamond-bright stars. "A penny for your thoughts," he said when she was silent for a long time.

"I was just thinking that I had a wonderful Christmas this year when I didn't expect to at all."

The boy gave her mittened hand a squeeze that seemed to say, "I'm so glad, and I know it wasn't easy."

The final word on the day was spoken by Molly in drowsy tones when Janet crawled in under the comforter beside her. "It seemed like *she* was here."

Chapter XVII

A Woodshed Warming

"People have housewarmings. Why don't we have a woodshed warming?" asked Janet. "Anyway, this isn't just a woodshed."

It was summer again and a good summer for the family on the little hillside farm. The rain had fallen when it was needed, and the sun had shone when it should shine. The potatoes, the strawberries, and the raspberries—in fact, all the fruits and vegetables—had yielded abundantly. The railroad ties hewn out of the chestnut trees in the pasture had been sold for a good price to the railroad company. Free'n'Equal had a handsome daughter. The drought of last summer and the winter's gale seemed to have happened a long time ago in some other unfriendly world. Now on the foundations of the old woodshed, a bright new building stood.

It seemed to the girl that only by putting on a neighborhood celebration could she express how happy she was.

"Why, sure," agreed Mr. Bradley. "Invite some of the young folks in."

"I mean young folks, old folks, kids—a kind of neighborhood party. I'd like to ask everybody in the Roaring Brook School district. Let's see, that would be the Clarks and the Millers and—oh yes, the Duboises."

"Those Canucks?" asked Mr. Bradley doubtfully. "Why, they can't talk English."

"They're our neighbors, and I went to school with Marie and Napoleon. And there's one more person I want to ask—Ed Cowing, even if he does live in the Center, because it's his woodshed."

"If you think you can mix so many kinds of folks together and give them a good time, go ahead. But don't bite off more than you can chew. And how would you get them all into the woodshed?"

"I wouldn't. Some would sit in the parlor and talk. Some would play quiet games in the sitting room, and the rest would play noisy games in the woodshed. We could move the organ out there."

This new shed was a joy to the entire family. Mr. Bradley remembered the snow he had shoveled out of the old building, with its front open to the weather, and smiled at the thought of the winter's wood supply being kept dry. Molly ran about, squatting here and there like a small toad, to pick up fascinating blocks of wood left by Ed Cowing's saw. There were cubes and pyramids and oblongs, perfect for building miniature houses and sheds and barns for a doll establishment. Dick immediately picked out a corner and appropriated it for a between-season resting place when it was too hot behind the kitchen stove and too cool under the lilac bush in the yard.

To Janet, it was much more than a woodshed. That room, with large windows shut off from the rest of the building by a partition, was her future workshop. Sometimes she would take a kitchen chair out there and peel potatoes or shell peas or sew just for the fun of being in a place that already seemed like her own.

What a lot of talking she had had to do before her father could see any sense in her plan! What did she want with a workshop now? She would be in school next fall and wouldn't have any time to work in it. How did she know she'd ever need a big place like this?

His questions brought the girl up short. Why, she couldn't give up this business of hers now or ever. It had become tremendously important to her—something she loved to do just for the sake of doing it. She felt about making wreaths and ropes of green the way some people felt about painting pictures or playing the piano.

"I shall work Saturdays and Teachers' Convention Day and Cattle Show Day and Thanksgiving vacation," she told her father. "Then, as soon as I graduate, I'm going to have a big business with a lot of folks working for me. It would be much more expensive to put an addition on later."

Finally, after she had talked and talked, Mr. Bradley enlarged his idea of the new building. "It'll come in handy for a storeroom anyway," he said. His daughter was silent, but she had no intention of seeing this place cluttered up with rakes and hoes, berry baskets, apple barrels, and goodness knows what else.

The old carpenter thought it was the "fanciest woodshed" he had ever built. Janet sat down amidst the shavings and told the old man about the things she hoped to do in this room.

Janet delivered the invitations to the woodshed warming in person on a Saturday afternoon, beginning at the Clarks' and ending at a small white cottage in the woods near Roaring Brook Falls. The broad-bosomed, black-eyed woman who came to the door looked at her suspiciously, shook her head, and said the three English words she knew, "No speak English." She understood the invitation no better than did the baby who came creeping across the kitchen floor behind her, and perhaps not so well.

A bright patch of color appeared at the edge of the cornfield, and Marie came on a run across the small clearing, her black pigtails and the gold crescents in her ears swinging in quick time. In less than a minute, all five of the half-grown members of the Dubois family had seemingly risen out of the ground and were standing around Janet, grinning. Marie spoke something in French to her mother. Mrs. Dubois smiled but shrugged her shoulders.

There wasn't any doubt of the Matthews coming—all ten of them, from old Gramp to four-year-old Eileen. The invitation produced a state of hilarious anticipation in the little old story-and-a-half house that sagged on its sills like an overloaded ship.

"I guess everybody that can speak English will be here," Janet reported with satisfaction to her father and Molly.

The first to arrive on the following Saturday night was, characteristically enough, Grandpa Matthews. He limped into the yard before the girls had finished washing and wiping the supper dishes. "By gad! There's no telling at all when the young ones and their Ma will get here, with all the scrubbing and prinking up they're doing this night," he gave warning. Mr. Bradley promptly lured him to the barn and engaged him in a heated discussion of the tariff. Meanwhile, as soon as the work in the kitchen was done, Janet arranged Molly's curls and helped her fasten the out-of-reach buttons at the back of her pink and white gingham. By the time the other nine Matthews arrived, she too had finished prinking. Her hair was braided and doubled up. She had on her cherry-colored dress, and the silver bangles jingled on her arm.

There were any number of surprises that evening. Surprise number one, the Dubois family all came. Mrs. Dubois, who understood none of the chatter around her except when her man Joe acted as interpreter, nevertheless seemed to have a thoroughly good time. Her sun-browned face was crinkled into a perpetual smile, and her beady eyes missed nothing that went on. Surprise number two was that Joe brought his accordion and responded willingly to requests to sing French songs. Surprise number three was that the older guests had no desire to sit in the parlor and talk. They crowded into the woodshed and around the organ to join the young folks in singing "Juanita," "Spanish Cavalier," and "O My Darling Clementine" and even made a pretense of humming the latest ragtime songs. Places had to be found at the long table for Grandpa Matthews and Ed Cowing when the boys and girls started a game of Up Jenkins.

Another rather disconcerting surprise was the amount of refreshments consumed. Three times Janet brewed a new supply of coffee in the great tin pot borrowed from the church kitchen. Of all that array of cakes she had baked, at least one of which she had expected to have left for family use, only a single piece remained. Before she had finished gathering up the empty plates, Grandpa Matthews slipped this off the plate and into his mouth after offering it to everyone about him with elaborate politeness.

Anyway, the experiment of mixing so many kinds of people together and giving them a good time was a success. You had only to look around at their faces to know that.

"Ain't had so much fun since Deacon Bates had his barn raising twenty years ago," declared Gramp.

"I wish somebody else would build a new woodshed soon," Etta Hastings remarked wistfully.

In the spare room, when the women and girls were putting on hats and "fascinators," Mrs. Matthews drew Janet into a corner. "I've had the loveliest time," she told her. "I felt like a girl again going to parties and barn dances." The woman's eyes sparkled as if she were actually reliving those evenings of her girlhood. Locks of hair, escaping from the others that were strained tight back into her pug, curled round her lined, tired face.

"Why, she must have been actually pretty once," Janet decided.

"Ed Cowing says that big room in the new shed is a kind of workshop for you and that you're going to hire a lot of folks to make laurel wreaths and things—and—I wondered if you couldn't use me and Emma."

"Well, not this year, I guess, but I'm going to have a big business like that someday."

"You mean—you mean—you won't be needing *any* help this year?"

"I hardly think so. You see, I'm going back to high school in September, so I won't try to fill many orders this year."

"Oh-h-h! I see." Again she was dull-eyed—an old woman with seven children.

"If I do need help," the girl added quickly, "I'll certainly call on you and Emma first."

"I wish you would. I do wish you would. You see, it's on account of Ben. The doctor says he'll never run and play like the other children till he's had an operation on his hip, but he can't have it unless we can find some way to make extra money. Well, goodnight."

Nobody had wanted to go home. There was only half-hearted talk about leaving till almost ten, and it was close to eleven before the last goodnight had been said and the last lantern had sent a glimmering, shifting path of light down the dark hill road.

As for Janet, she had had a wonderful time at her own party. There had been no opportunity to chatter with her own special friends; she'd hardly spoken a dozen words with Mary or Steve or the Millers. For refreshments, she had swallowed a few sips of coffee and half a slice of cake between refilling plates and cups. Yet it had all been fun.

There were just two blots on the evening's happiness. One was the way Mrs. Matthews had looked when she'd said, "Oh-h-h." The other was the envy in Ben's eyes as he had sat and watched the other youngsters play Blind Man's Bluff. At twelve, a boy ought not to be lame, ought not to be watching other people play.

Life would be a whole heap simpler, she thought, if what she did and didn't do wasn't always affecting someone else—Molly, her father, and now even Ben Matthews. Why in the world did Ed Cowing have to blab about her affairs anyway? Next time, she'd keep her mouth shut when he was around.

Chapter XVIII

The Telegram Was Important

Janet's annoyance at the old carpenter's wagging tongue increased the next morning when Etta Hastings brought a note from her mother. It read—

Dear Janet:
I won't have the schoolteacher to board next fall, because Lilly Evans from the Center is going to be the new teacher, and she'll drive back and forth. It's the first time in ten years that I couldn't count on that board money, and I'm going to miss it terrible even if Etta works steady for you. I hear you are going to do a big business in Christmas greens this year. Don't you want some help? I'm sure I could make nice wreaths. Folks always say I have a real knack with my fingers.
Yours truly,
Mrs. Henry Hastings

"Ma said I was to wait for an answer," said Etta.

Janet was silent for a long time. She wasn't looking at Etta, who stood in the yard waiting a little impatiently, or at the note in her hand. Her eyes rested dreamily on the dark green crown of the hill.

"Tell your mother," she said finally, just as the bearer of the letter had decided that Janet couldn't have heard what she said, "tell her that I may need some help. I'll let her know."

"Oh! She'll be so glad if you do. She's awful upset about the teacher's living at home."

"Now whatever did I say that for?" she asked herself as she watched Etta's dark-blue-calico-clad figure retreat down the hill. "Why get her hopes up for nothing?"

Again the girl's glance wandered up the hill, then back to the woodshed.

The last two weeks of August were packed full of preparations for the beginning of school. Janet drove to Eastbrook with Molly and bought new shoes for them. She took her old fall coat to Grace Miller, the village dressmaker, to have the sleeves cut over and the worn velvet collar replaced with a new one. There was still plenty of sewing left for her to do at home. She ripped up her old brown serge dress, discarded the worn part, and made a new dress for Molly out of the remainder; put a new yoke into her own plaid dress; and mended stockings, and stockings, and stockings.

The whole house was cleaned from cellar to attic. "I'm not going to have Etta telling folks that I'm a slack housekeeper," said Janet, for she well knew that Etta's favorite amusement was to peddle among the neighbors gossip about the women whom she helped out from time to time. So Janet worked early and late scrubbing floors and buttery shelves, scouring the black stains of wood smoke off the bottoms of kettles, and polishing the small glass panes of the windows. She even cleaned the back chamber where the fragrance of last year's Christmas greens still lingered. How happy those days spent in this room had been, she thought, while she swept bits of laurel and pine out of the corners.

Early one morning as she sat balanced on the sill of one of the front windows, Homer Snow came driving up to the door. For a breathless moment, she thought he was bringing unexpected company. It was one of Homer's numerous odd jobs to drive passengers to and from the depot. No. The back seat of the long, covered carriage was empty. At the sight of the yellow envelope in his hand, a worse panic seized her, and she almost fell over backward. In her experience, a telegram meant just one kind of news—bad news. Could Grandma or Grandpa be sick—or worse?

"You don't have to be scared to open it," he reassured her. "George said it didn't seem to be very important, and I needn't hurry about driving up with it—something to do with those Christmas greens you make. As George says, it's a mighty long time between now and next Christmas, but I thought I might as well come along with it now.

"Any answer?" he asked finally, after the girl had stood staring at the message for fully three minutes.

"No. Not now. I've got to do a lot of thinking before I answer it."

"Well," muttered Homer to his horse as he drove home, "she sure acted like that telegram *was* important."

Tucking the yellow paper into the pocket of her apron, Janet left the window she had been washing half-bright and half-cloudy and started for the hilltop woods to do "a lot of thinking." She was glad she was alone today, glad there was no one to ask questions. Mr. Bradley had left at dawn on the long drive to Northbrook with a load of potatoes and wouldn't be back till suppertime, and Molly was spending the day with Phoebe Clark. This was her problem, and she wanted to settle it alone.

Not till she was lying under the big pine tree by the spring did she take the telegram from her pocket. The message read—

CAN YOU SUPPLY ONE THOUSAND YARDS OF LAUREL ROPE BY SEPTEMBER TWENTY-FOURTH? WIRE REPLY.

MOORE AND SMOLLET

A thousand yards! How could she say "no"? If she hustled and got this special order off promptly, then Moore & Smollet would be sure to want another big order filled for Christmas. Yet how could she possibly say "yes"? It would mean working by daylight and by lamplight and hiring the neighbors to help her. And it meant—that she would not be among those present when the Eastbrook High School opened!

Janet knew just what her father would say, and he would be right, she supposed. "Sorry. Cannot fill order." That would have to be her answer. Anyway, there was no need of sending it yet. After dinner, she would go down to the Warrens' and ask if she might use their telephone, and she would call up George Weeks at the depot and give him that message. He would send it click-clicking over the wires more than a hundred miles, and he wouldn't think it important. How little he knew!

A long streamer of trailing pine reached out toward her across the brown needles. Just above the spring, a clump of shiny-leaved laurel caught the sunlight. The girl leaned back against the tree trunk and shut her eyes. She could see her new shop with a long table in it and women and girls working around the table. Men and boys would be driving into the yard with loads of green treasure and would pile heaps of it on the floor. Those heaps would melt like snow drifts in May. There would be laughter and talk. Perhaps Mrs. Matthews would smile that young smile again and say she hadn't had such a good time since she was a girl. And in the kitchen, Etta would be cooking and washing dishes and singing at the top of her voice.

Something warm and moist tickled her palm. Dick, who had hunted her up, stood licking her hand. He waited for her to stroke his head, but she just fingered the spray of ground pine and looked into space.

"All right, old fellow," she cried, "I'll race you to the house."

Off they went down the hill, out of the woods into the

sunshine, along the wall through goldenrod and asters, skirting the strawberry bed, the dug-over potato patch, and a field of tasseled corn. Dick, who had started out at an easy trot, was soon making great leaps to keep ahead of the flying figure behind him. What had happened to his mistress? Had she grown wings? Would she at any moment now go skimming along over his head with the swallows?

Stephen Warren sat on the porch of the Warren farmhouse, his head bent low over a book. Not till her step sounded on the gravel driveway did he see Janet. Then he stared at her for a moment as if she were a stranger. She had forgotten to take off the bibbed, blue-checked apron she had put on when she started to wash windows. There was a dark smudge on one cheek. All the short locks of her hair had escaped and were curling around her face. Her cheeks were fiery, though the day was cool.

"Can I use your telephone, Stephen?" she called out before he had time even to say hello.

"What's wrong, Janet? What's happened? You look as if you'd been to a fire."

"Nothing's wrong. Everything's wonderful."

"Want me to get the number for you?"

"Will you, please? It always scares me to turn that crank. I want to get the depot."

He followed her into the dining room, took down the receiver from the wooden box fastened to the wall, listened a minute, then hung up again.

"You won't get the depot for fifteen minutes probably. Mrs. Miller is reading to Mrs. Hayes a letter she just got from her cousin Sadie, and I wouldn't wonder if that letter was ten pages long. Come out on the porch and help me cram Roman history for college entrance exams."

Janet perched on the edge of a porch chair and wondered impatiently how long she would have to wait.

"Just think," began Stephen eagerly, "in four weeks I'll be a freshman at Amherst. I'm going to live in South College, and I've had a letter from Grover Williams, the fellow that's going to be my roommate. He comes clear from Cleveland, Ohio—think of that—and he plays a banjo and was on his high school baseball team. I guess there ain't no flies on him."

"That's fine, Steve. That's wonderful," said the girl absently, then asked, "Do you suppose the line is still busy?"

***

"I want to send a telegram," she announced importantly when a loud "hello" from Mr. Weeks came over the wire. Stephen and his mother and grandmother, both of whom appeared suddenly from the kitchen just as Janet began to telephone, were mystified by the message they heard repeated twice into the mouthpiece: "Will fill order by September twenty-fourth. Signed, Janet Bradley."

Refusing an invitation to "sit down and stay a while," Janet started for home. "Wait a minute, I'll walk along with you," said Stephen.

"When do you take that exam?" she asked, knowing perfectly well that the boy walking beside her wanted to ask questions instead of answering them.

"Week after next." He stopped short, scuffed the dusty road for a moment with one toe, then asked bluntly, "Why all the mystery about that telegram?"

"It's no mystery. I've just had a big order for laurel roping to be filled in a hurry, and I'm going to fill it. That's all."

"But how can you and go to school, too?"

"I'm not going to school. I'll just study a while longer and get the Roaring Brook school teacher to tutor me some and let it go at that."

"Wha-at? And I thought you were so ambitious."

"I am. I'm probably more ambitious than any girl in Glenbrook, only my ambitions are different. Can't you understand, Steve?" she asked earnestly. "It's like Cousin Anna said—a person can be educated and yet not have much schooling. I'm getting one kind of education right on Laurel Hill, and I believe I've a chance to be as useful here as I could be anywhere else in the world."

"You don't mean you want to stay here in a dead hole like Glenbrook on a farm all the rest of your life?"

"Yes, I've just decided that's exactly what I do want to do."

"Oh!"

Neither could seem to think of anything else to say, and presently, even before he reached "halfway knoll," the boy decided that he must get back to his history book. "Well, good luck." The tone of his voice implied that he didn't see how his wish for her could possibly come true.

"Good luck to you!"

She turned round to wave her hand from the bend in the road, but the boy did not look back.

"He didn't understand what I was talking about any more than if I were jabbering Polish or Italian," she thought, "and we used to feel the same way about pretty near everything."

Chapter XIX

Return of a Gold Miner

Janet stopped at her house only long enough to finish polishing the half-washed window, wash the smudges off her face, and eat a bowl of bread and milk. Then she was off again down the hill toward Roaring Brook. This time her first stop was at the Millers' house under the hill.

"We'll have our bikes! We'll have our bikes!" Delia and Roy Miller jumped up and down in the kitchen till the dishes rattled on the shelves, the stove poker fell off the stove, and their mother said she couldn't hear herself think and begged them to keep quiet or go outdoors. "We've been getting folks to subscribe to the *Youth's Companion*, and when we have five more subscriptions apiece and ten dollars, they'll send us the most beautiful bicycles you ever saw in your life," Roy explained. "Wait a minute, and I'll show you a picture of them," offered Delia, running into the sitting room. Janet could not take time to wait for the magazine to be hunted up, much to the disappointment of the young Millers. She warned them that they probably would not make enough money this fall to finish paying for bicycles, but they did not seem to hear her. In their imaginations, the bicycles were practically paid for.

There was no answer to her knock at the Hastings' back

door, but presently a voice called from the yard, and Mrs. Hastings appeared from out of a tangle of blackberry vines with a tin pail in her hand.

"Can you come Monday to my house and learn to make laurel roping and work for me for two or three weeks, and can Etta come too and do the housework?" asked the girl.

The tin pail dropped to the ground as if the firm hand that held it had turned to jelly. "Well, I never! Well, I never!" the older woman exclaimed over and over in surprised delight, while the two of them kneeled on the ground and began picking up the scattered berries.

It wasn't necessary to knock at the Matthews' door. Minnie, the next to the youngest of the children, was picking up a basket of chips by the chopping block in the yard. At the sight of the visitor, she started on a run for the house, calling, "Ma! Ma!" Jimmy, teetering up and down with Mary on a plank laid across a sawhorse, let his small sister drop to the ground with dangerous suddenness and ran after Minnie, as if he wanted to be the first to announce Janet's arrival.

Mrs. Matthews appeared at the back door with Eileen. Mr. Matthews, in the potato patch behind the house, leaned on his hoe and listened. Gramp arose from his chair under the maple tree and came across the yard to see what was going on, and Emma and Sam ran from the garden with a basket of shell beans—all of them at almost the same moment. A caller was an exciting event at their house.

Janet delivered her message. Mrs. Matthews' smile was a joy to see. "May the saints bless you!" she exclaimed fervently. "Emma and I'll be up to your house tomorrow, bright and early, and Jimmy and Sam can begin picking laurel this afternoon, if you want them to."

"Remember," the girl cautioned the two boys, "don't skin all the branches and leaves off the laurel bushes. Leave enough on every one so that your green treasure will keep on growing.

I'll show you what I mean." She gave a demonstration of laurel conservation, using the elderberry bush by the door for the lesson.

As she went on her way, Janet noticed that Ben was lying in a hammock at the side of the house and that his great dark eyes were fixed on her.

Halfway up the road on the way home, she saw Marie and Napoleon Dubois coming toward her down the road carrying pails of blackberries. "I'll ask them to pick, too," she decided quickly.

Marie's earrings bobbed up and down hilariously. "Yes, sure," she said. Napoleon's eyes were like polished black shoe buttons. "Maybe we get a good horse," he anticipated optimistically. "That one we got is just a—a—" He stopped and wrinkled his tanned forehead.

"Nag," said Marie triumphantly, proud of knowing an English word her brother couldn't remember.

"I certainly feel like Santa Claus," thought Janet. Only she did wish that everybody didn't expect to make such a lot of money right away and buy bicycles and horses and cure lame boys in a few weeks.

She came out of the woods and looked up the slope to the house to see if her father or Molly had come home. On the side porch stood a man, but it was not Mr. Bradley. He was knocking persistently at the door as if determined to rouse someone. He looked like a tramp!

The girl dodged quickly behind one of the maple trees by the roadside and watched him. She was not afraid of strange dogs or of snakes or of many people, but she was afraid of tramps. So she waited, screened by the broad tree trunk, for the man to stop hammering at her door and go on his way. He had stopped. He was leaving. No, he was just looking up and down the road. O dear! O dear! He was sitting down on the porch. If only Papa would come home. Why didn't Dick growl

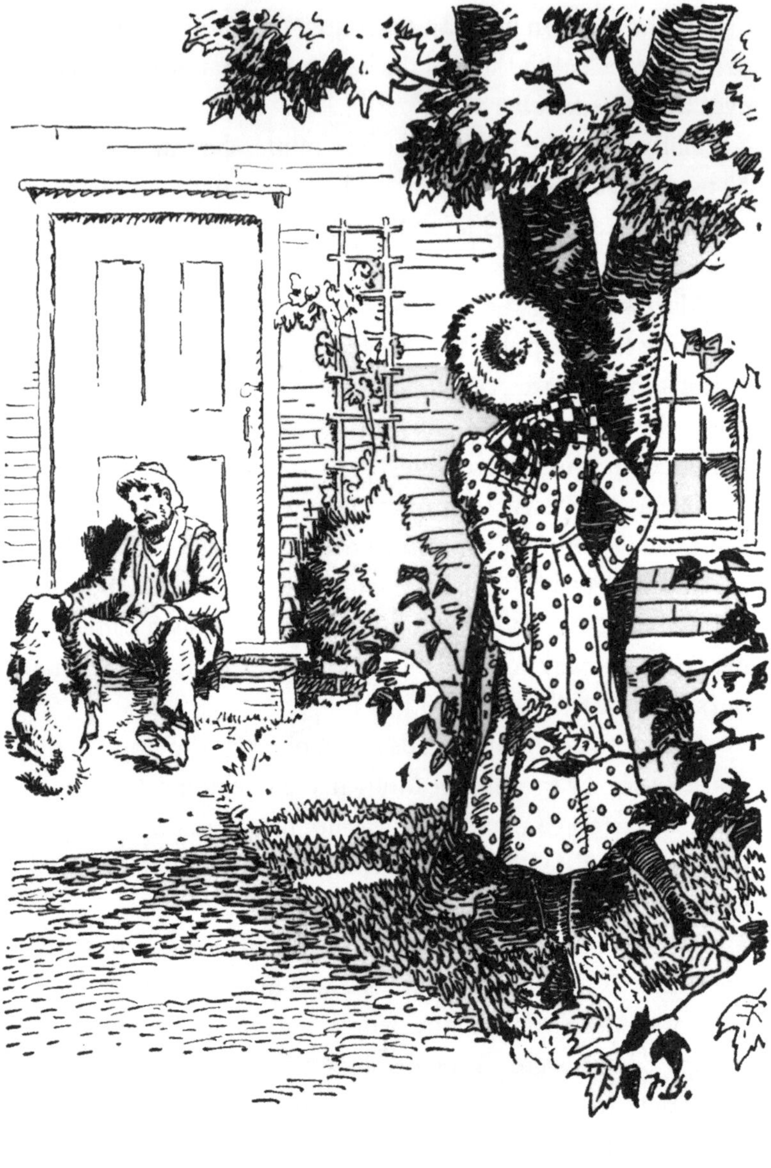

and bark instead of lying right down at that disreputable man's feet? Was he getting too old to have any spunk?

She began to think of all the stories she had heard about tramps. Sometimes they broke into people's houses. One had once tried to set fire to the Hastings' barn out of spite when Mrs. Hastings refused to give him something to eat. Suppose—suppose this tramp should set fire to the new woodshed! Trying to look bold and fearless, she jumped up and walked quickly toward the house while the tramp sat and watched her. To the girl's surprise, he stood up and pulled off his cap politely when she came within speaking distance.

"Why if it ain't little Janet all grown up!" he said. "Don't you remember me?"

She shook her head. And yet those black eyes did look somehow familiar.

"I'm Billy Hastings."

It couldn't be Billy. Not this ragged, bearded man who looked as if he had slept for weeks with his clothes on. He was too old to be Billy anyway. Then he smiled. She recognized him and felt unhappy and did not know what to say.

Six—or was it seven years ago—he had said goodbye to them all right here and had gone swaggering off, bragging of the gold he would bring back from the Klondike. "I'll bring you a nugget as big as your curly head," he had told Janet. He had sent some small gold nuggets back to his mother, which she, beaming proudly, had exhibited to all the neighbors. They were real gold, and everybody said they guessed Billy had "struck it rich." People kept asking Mrs. Hastings when he was coming home, but she never heard from him again, except for a card once a year that just said, "Merry Christmas, From Billy." So after a while, they stopped asking questions about him. Lulu Hatch, the postmistress, said that those cards were mailed every year from a different place out West. Only the first one had come from Alaska.

Janet still didn't know what to say to Billy when he was in the kitchen, sitting stiffly in a chair with his feet drawn under it so that the holes in his shoes wouldn't show. "I guess your mother was awful glad to see you," she said at last, to break the long, embarrassing silence. She wondered why Mrs. Hastings had been silent about this homecoming.

"Ma hasn't seen me yet."

"Oh!"

"I didn't want her to see me like this. I—I—thought—you folks were always so nice to me—I thought you'd let me spruce up a little here before I went home. So I hopped off the freight train when it slowed down at the brickyard and came here cross-lots."

After tactful, hesitating offers on the one side and embarrassed acceptances on the other, the tramp that was not a tramp retired to the woodshed with a towel, a wash basin, and a complete outfit of clothes borrowed from the closet in Mr. Bradley's bedroom.

Janet set out on the kitchen table some slices of bread, a pot of cottage cheese, and a pitcher of milk. He certainly looked hungry.

When he came into the kitchen again, with the soot washed off his neck and face and the stubble shaved from his cheeks and wearing a whole suit, he was recognizable as Billy Hastings, but a Billy who was much more tired and sober and old than the merry-eyed young man who had promised Janet a huge nugget of gold. At the sight of the food on the table, such a ravenous look came into his eyes that Janet hastily added some thick hunks of cold corned beef.

The girl had never seen anybody eat the way he did—with such fierce intensity. Why, he was like Cappy, the Clarks' hound when he came home that time after he'd been lost for days on Pitcher Mountain.

As if reading her thoughts, Billy looked up presently and said, "Guess I've et like a hunting dog, but I ain't had any women-cooked victuals for years, and—well—as a matter of fact—the last bit of food I had was yesterday noon. They don't have dining cars for the fellers that ride the bumpers," he added with a twisted smile.

"Sometimes I used to dream I was eating a meal of Ma's victuals," he went on, "and it seemed like I'd give my right arm to make that dream come true."

"But why didn't you come home?" Janet asked bluntly.

"First, I was ashamed to, till I could bring back the gold I said I'd be loaded with. And when I got desperate enough to swallow my pride, I didn't have any money to pay my way." A dark look was in his face, as if the mere thought of the years of hardship behind him cast a long shadow across the present. The girl decided to change the subject and began to talk about the business she had started. "He needs to keep awful busy for a while and feel as if he were mighty useful and not just a bum," she decided, then said, "Perhaps you'd like to work for me, picking laurel."

"Say, would you really like to have me help you?" He was pathetically eager.

"I sure would."

She stood on the porch and watched him go off down the road, turning again and again to wave to her, as if he were trying to express in motions the gratitude he had spoken haltingly.

"And all these years, I thought he was traveling around and having fun and living on the fat of the land," she said out loud. "And he's just as glad to get home as Cappy was."

Mr. Bradley looked across the supper table that night at his older daughter and thought he had never before seen such happy contentment in her face. "I guess," he said jokingly, "that you've been having a high old time while I've been away."

"I have," said Janet.

Chapter XX

Up a Dead-End Road

In October, Janet again set out to rally her forces along Roaring Brook. In high spirits, she hailed Delia and Roy as they raked leaves in their dooryard and told them about the two letters that had come within the last few days. One was from Moore & Smollet with an order for Christmas greens twice the size of last year's. The other had arrived quite unexpectedly from another florist, a firm she had written to in vain last year.

"I'm really in business now," Janet gloated, "and I shall want you two to pick lots of laurel for me."

Delia's forehead drew into criss-cross lines.

"But *where* are we going to find lots of laurel? We've picked our pasture clean; that is, as clean as we can and not hurt the plants."

Roy pushed the toe of his boot into the lawn and scuffed thoughtfully till the earth under it was brown and bare. They had added five dollars to their bicycle fund in September. Now here was a chance to earn the rest of the money if only they could find some more laurel.

Giving the ground a disgusted kick, the boy said, "I've a good mind to sneak up and pick in the old Stanley pasture and not say a word to anybody, even if old man Libbey has plastered it all over with signs. What's the sense in letting all that perfectly good laurel go to waste?"

"Oh! You mustn't." Janet looked worried. "He could fine you or have you put in the lockup if he caught you picking anything on his land, and I'll bet he would, too."

"Fat lot of good that stuff's doing him. He's just a dog in the manger—that's what he is."

"The laurel's his, just the same." Janet stared out across Roaring Brook Valley with eyes that saw not the red and gold leaves thrown out like banners against hemlocks and pines. "Maybe I'll—go—and—have a talk with him." The words came slowly. It was evident that the offer had been made not without a struggle. To ask a favor of that hairy, slit-eyed man was, in truth, the last thing she wanted to do.

She had scarcely seen him, except at a distance, since that day a year ago when he had warned her off his land, but she had heard nothing good about him in the meantime. His only interest in his neighbors seemed to be in borrowing their tools or getting the better of them in a trade.

Once out of sight of the Millers, Janet began kicking herself for having made the offer. Why was she jumping into this with both feet? Delia and Roy could ask their own favors. She'd tell them on the way home that they'd better see Mr. Libbey themselves.

Billy Hastings' long-legged, blue-jean-clad figure emerged from the lane leading to his pasture. "Jiminy!" he exclaimed. "You sure got up before breakfast this morning. I've only just turned the cows out.

"That's great," he said when she told him about her Christmas order. "I suppose that means you'll want Ma and Etta to work for you again."

"Yes, and I want you to pick for me."

Billy turned and looked up between the two stone walls

that marked the lane. "Well, I don't know about that. There ain't near so much laurel up there as I counted on. Used to be a sight of it, but the woods has growed up and choked it out. Have you got any more up to your place than you folks can take care of?"

She shook her head. "No more than Papa and Molly can easily pick. We used a lot last month, you know."

Oh dear! Oh dear! Had she been counting on green treasure that didn't exist? If only the Stanley place hadn't changed hands when she so needed the yield of its rocky hillside pasture!

It was Mrs. Matthews who, unconsciously to be sure, screwed Janet's courage to the sticking point. At the girl's announcement, her face took on that young, shiny-eyed look again. "The Lord's answered my prayers," she said fervently. "Ben's been feeling worse this fall. His hip hurts him bad, and I've been praying you'd want me to work for you a lot so's I could send him to the hospital right after Christmas. And Jimmy and Sam will pick laurel and pines for you." There was a singing quality in her voice. "There ain't much more to pick on our place, but I suppose there's slathers up on Laurel Hill, ain't there?"

"We'll find plenty for them," said Janet firmly and went quickly on her way.

Napoleon and Marie were rustling about under the big chestnut trees just below the house, picking out from the leaves the shiny brown nuts last night's heavy frost had released from the burs. At the sight of Janet, they stopped and came hippity-hop to meet her. For them, she was always a bringer of good tidings.

"That's just what we thought you'd want, Napoleon and me, when we see you coming," said Marie delightedly, after Janet had told them about her Christmas order.

Yes, they could begin picking for her right away—today.

Yes, there was still laurel and pine in their woods. Oh no! There wasn't any more than they could pick by themselves.

Instead of turning around and going home, Janet kept on past the Duboises' shack on the grass-grown road that led to Roaring Brook Falls and—to the Libbeys'.

"Going up to the falls?" Marie called after her.

"Yes."

Yet when she came to the opening in the woods where the brook roared and foamed over a wall of rock, the girl did not even stop to watch it tumble on the moss-grown stones below or look for wagtails bobbing up and down among the pools of water.

On she went through the deep woods, past an abandoned lumberjack's shack and a farmhouse that had long since fallen into a heap of silver and black timber. The road grew more grass-grown at every step and seemed to lead on and on into an endless wilderness. Even the mailman did not travel over it but left the Libbeys' mail at the Duboises' place. Once she stopped and looked around, as if weakening, then threw back her head, made a tight line out of her small mouth, and went on up the lonely road.

Once long ago, the "Falls Road" had continued on around Laurel Hill to the Center. Now it was a dead-end road, impassable beyond the Libbey place and traveled, except for picnic parties to the falls, only by the Libbeys and those who came to see them. How still it was in the woods! Not even crows or hawks seemed to live in this lonely place. Wasn't she ever going to get there? It would have been quicker to go back home and cut cross-lots over the hill, but she might as well keep on now.

A rooster's crowing broke the stillness. Through the thinning woods, the girl saw the plank-sided box of a house. They had shingled the house and built a chimney and had put up another ugly wooden box for a barn.

Out of the yard, a mongrel dog, half-hound half-shepherd,

came purposefully, eyeing the girl with suspicion and yelping something that sounded unfit for print. "Nice doggie! Nice doggie!" said Janet, determined not to let this cur know she was afraid of him. He was neither fooled nor soothed by this kind of talk, but curled up his lip to show a strong set of teeth and stood right in the gateway of the fence as if daring her to enter.

It was all she could do at this point to keep from leaving this forlorn place and its ugly watchdog. Perhaps only the thought of how silly she would look turning tail and going back the way she had come made her stand her ground and call loudly, "Hello! Hello!"

"Teddy! Shush, or I'll whale the hide off you!" The snarling man sounded more unpleasant than the snarling dog.

"Well, if it ain't Jim Bradley's girl, come to see us." From the barn emerged the man she and Molly had met on the hill a year ago. The voice was suave but unpleasant—what Janet called a "castor-oil voice." The lips were smiling, but the eyes were as unfriendly as the dog's.

"Ma, Minnie, Sophy," he called in the direction of the house, "you got company."

Instantly, as if waiting for a signal, a middle-aged woman and two girls came to the door and peered out. At the same time, Janet was conscious of a boy lurking behind the open barn door. This was the boy who wasn't quite bright, she supposed. They all reminded her of animals peering out of their holes.

"I—I'm afraid I can't stop," she said quickly, "I just wanted to speak to you about something." Was that faint voice her own?

"Come right in and set down," urged Mr. Libbey with a mock heartiness, ignoring her protest.

She followed him across the yard and stepped over the board set across the doorsill to keep the chickens from wandering in and out.

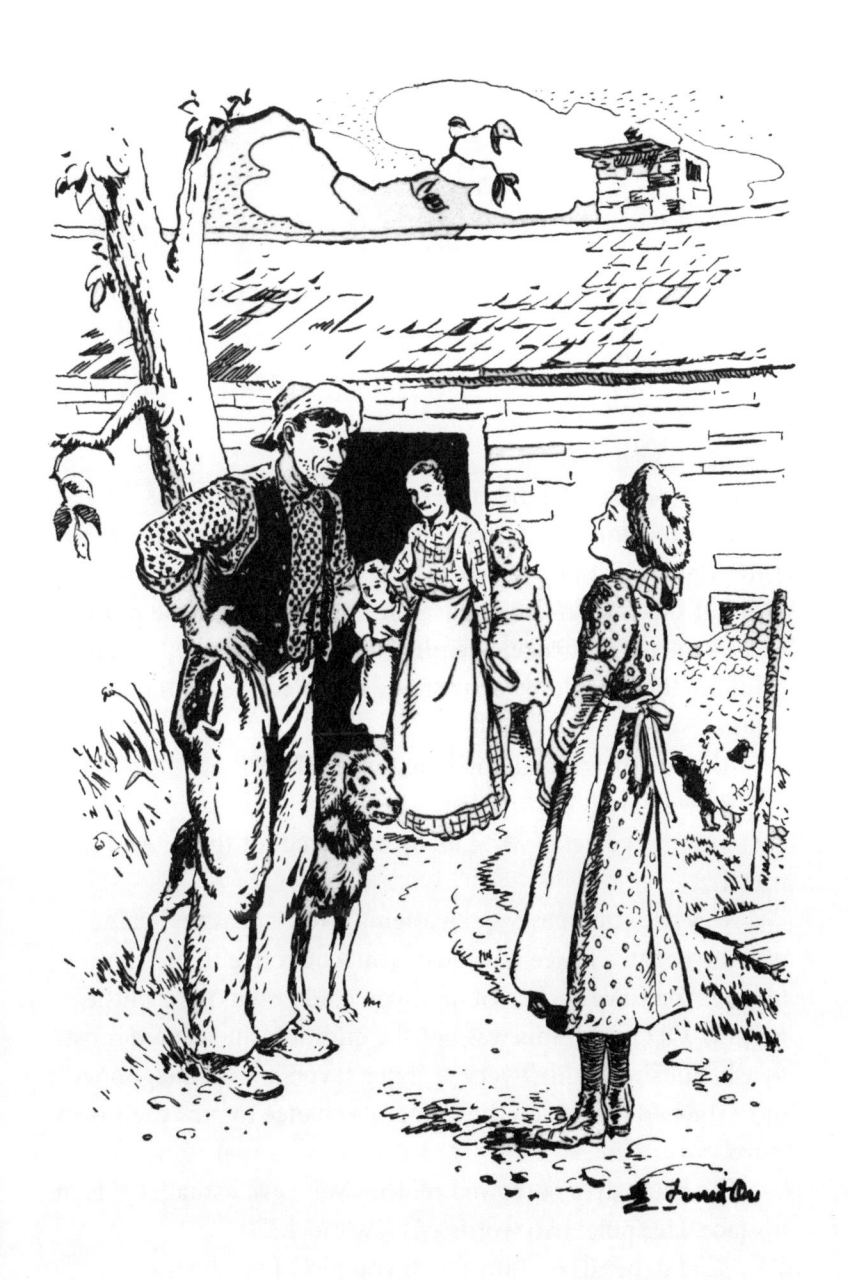

Chapter XXI

Dog in the Manger

Janet perched on the edge of a chair in a kitchen as littered and uncared-for as the dooryard. The four Libbeys sat silently. Their four pairs of eyes were fastened on her. It seemed to the girl as if she couldn't open her mouth, and yet that she must break that awful silence. She turned hopefully to the two girls, thinking they would be easier to talk to than their father and mother.

"Do you girls like living here?" she asked.

They giggled.

"Sure they like it," Mr. Libbey answered for them. And that was that.

Now the guest gave up all attempts to be chatty. "I came up," she began, "to see if some of you would like to pick laurel for me. You have such a lot of it, you could earn quite a little money." Of course, this was not the question she wanted most to ask, but she couldn't very well beg favors for the neighbors until she had first given the Libbeys a chance to pick their own laurel.

The man's eyes narrowed till they were even smaller slits in his face. He spoke two words—"How much?"

"That depends on how much you pick. I pay by the pound—two cents a pound."

He grinned slyly. "Quite a game, ain't it?"

The girls giggled. The woman's face was expressionless.

"What do you mean?" asked Janet with dignity.

"I mean you're making a pretty good thing out of this, ain't you? Getting the backwoods folks on Roaring Brook to pick cheap and selling your stuff for city prices. Bet you couldn't get none of the Center folks to pick for that."

Hot blood surged up into the girl's face. To be told she drove a hard bargain was the last thing she'd ever expected. By making a tremendous effort, she managed to keep her voice from trembling with anger. "Mr. Libbey, I'm not making a 'pretty good thing' out of this business. I'm paid wholesale, not retail prices, and work very hard for what I get. If it were possible to pay my pickers more, I'd gladly do it. As for the Center folks, I've never asked them to work for me because I want to give my neighbors first chance. Perhaps if you folks don't think it worth your while to pick, you'd be willing that the Matthews boys and some of the other neighbors pick in your pasture. They wouldn't make any trouble, and they wouldn't pick too clean. There'd be plenty left to grow another year."

The mere mention of sharing anything with others caused the man to shake his head and declare that he didn't want folks "tromping over his land and knocking down his fences."

Janet could hardly keep from laughing at this, for the fences were already so full of gaps that all summer the cattle had wandered up and down the road and even over the hill, through the woods, and down into her father's mowing.

"What do you say, Minnie and Sophy?" he asked. "Do you want to earn *a lot of money*?"

Again the visitor's cheeks burned at the mocking tone in which the question was asked.

"Ye-ah," they chorused and then burst out giggling afresh.

"How about you, Bud?" The question was put to the boy, who had been standing outside within earshot.

"Sure. I want to make a lot of money." The answer ended with a foolish laugh.

Were they all just making sport of her? she asked herself.

"Good!" she said aloud. "Can you begin right away? This week?"

"Sure, right away," said Mr. Libbey suavely.

"How about bringing me a wagonload Saturday?"

"That'll be fine and dandy," the head of the family agreed.

The girl started back down the road. It would have been much shorter to go home cross-lots over the hill, but she wanted to keep off Mr. Libbey's land. A gust of wind followed her, picking up the leaves from the ground and sending them to dance along ahead of her and bringing to her ears a burst of laughter from the door of the cottage under the hill. She walked as fast as she could without breaking into a run until the woods hid her; then she took to her heels and did not stop for breath until she could see the back of the Duboises' shack. She felt the way she used to when she was a little girl and Mother would send her down to the cellar. The dark corners were not so very fearsome as long as she was down there, but always she had to run upstairs because of that panicky feeling that something might jump out of the dimness and grab her when her back was turned. Yes, she felt very much as if she had been down in a dark cellar.

How good the friendly faces of Napoleon and Marie looked to her! She greeted them as if days had passed since they had met, instead of half an hour. Not till the bridge was reached was she calm enough to sit down and think things over. There was no chance of finding laurel enough around here to keep all her neighbors busy. Even though there was more laurel in the Libbey pasture than the whole family could pick in an entire year, Mr. Libbey would never share it with anyone. Of that she was certain. Well, Delia and Roy would probably have to wait for their bicycles, but Ben Matthews was *not* going to wait to be cured. She would have to give his mother extra work making wreaths, even if that would cut down on her own profits. Billy Hastings had to be kept busy, too, or he'd get an "itching foot" again and hop a freight train in search of excitement. She could manage all right, if only the Libbeys would keep their promise to supply her with laurel. Surely they wouldn't be quite so mean as neither to pick for her nor to let anybody else pick.

"Oh yes! Yes! I'll come to work for you every day. Yes, I can begin Monday." Mrs. Matthews was ecstatic. "Ain't it wonderful you're going to have such a lot for me to do this year?" She did not suspect that Janet was making work for her. Neither did Billy Hastings, when she stopped and asked if she could count on him next month to come up two or three days a week and help pack and nail up barrels. Yet, when she had gone on up the hill, he took off his cap and scratched his head thoughtfully. "Somehow she didn't look happy—like the way she generally does," he remarked to the hens scratching in the yard.

Janet was glad that Delia and Roy were nowhere to be seen about their place. She was suddenly tired out, as if she had been walking against a great wind.

On Saturday afternoon, she began watching the road for the Libbeys' horse and wagon. Even after supper, when the road had dimmed to a mere light streak through the darkness, she looked out every few minutes and listened intently whenever the rattle of wheels or the clop-clop of hoofs was heard outside.

The Libbeys had probably picked all the afternoon and couldn't get around to deliver it tonight. She was sure, so she pretended to herself, that a load of laurel would be in the yard on Monday, bright and early.

Monday dawned, but no wagonload of laurel came up the hill road. Just before milking time, Mr. Bradley offered to end Janet's uncertainty by driving over to the Libbey place. The sight of his daughter running hopefully to the window every time someone passed was getting on his nerves. Her face was an open book when she was disappointed. "If they've picked any laurel, I'll bring it home, and if they haven't, I'll give them a piece of my mind," he promised her.

In a surprisingly short time, he was home again with an empty wagon, without even having given his neighbor a piece of his mind. "I didn't see anybody but that boy," he reported disgustedly, "and he kept saying, 'I don't know, I don't know,' to every question I asked him, like a doggoned parrot that's learned just three words. Betcha anything that the whole family was there, hiding up like a lot of rabbits and letting him talk for them, if you call that talking. I was almost certain I heard voices before I came out of the woods."

Janet remembered the burst of mocking laughter that had followed her departure that day. Had the Libbeys just been stringing her along? By the time the week had passed, she knew the answer to her question was "Yes."

"Now what am I going to do?" she asked herself over and over again. She went up on the hill to take stock anew of her own treasure. There were plenty of ferns and ground pine. The laurel, with what the neighbors could still bring, would just about fill her orders from Moore & Smollet. That left practically none for the laurel wreaths ordered by the New York florist. Must she turn down this chance to expand her business? What was the use of getting such a good start if she couldn't go on filling larger orders each year, building up a reputation for herself among florists? Those bright dreams of hers for the future—not only of the Bradley family but of a whole neighborhood—were they to be only dreams? Oh, there had to be a way out, there *had* to be!

Coming back down the hill, she walked so slowly that Dick gave up trying to coax her into a romp with him and trotted off disgustedly by himself.

> *"We shall come, rejoicing,*
> *Bringing in the sheaves."*

Etta's shrill voice pealed out from the kitchen.

> *"Hark! the herald angels sing,"*

—Mrs. Matthews announced in her thin soprano, as if working on laurel wreaths had filled her mind even in October with thoughts of Christmas.

Janet did not feel this morning like joining in a song or like talking to her cheerful helpers. She stopped at the barn to gather eggs. Coming out into the yard a few minutes later, she was just in time to see Mr. Libbey climb the wall between the backyard and the mowing and slouch toward her.

"Mornin'," he said with disarming amiability.

The girl, thinking how much she would like to pick one of the eggs out of her apron and let it fly, forced the shadow of a smile to her lips and asked politely, "Won't you come in, Mr. Libbey?"

To her regret, he accepted the invitation. Sprawled out on her father's favorite rocking chair in the sitting room, he took a long time about cutting a piece of tobacco from his plug and stowing it away in his mouth.

"Sorry I wasn't home when your Pa come up last Monday," he began finally, after having had the satisfaction of watching Janet fidget impatiently in her chair. "The fact is, I don't see how my young-uns are going to git around to picking laurel. Their Ma and me, we keep them so busy. But when it comes to a neighbor, I always try to be accommodating. So I'm a-going to make you an offer. What do you say, young lady, to you and me going into partnership in this Christmas-greens business? You can have all the laurel and stuff you want to pick off my pasture if you give me half what you git for it."

For a moment, Janet did not let herself answer. Her only hope of getting any cooperation from this man was to keep her temper. When she did speak, her voice was quiet and controlled. "I'm afraid that wouldn't be a partnership. You see, what I pay people for laurel is only a part of my expenses. I have to buy cord and wire and steel hoops for making the ropes and wreaths and for wiring ferns into bunches, and packing cases to ship them in. Then there's freight to pay, and cold-storage charges, and wages to the women that come and help me in the shop. However, I'll be glad to give you a fair sum for the privilege of picking on your land."

"I'm nothing if not obliging when it comes to neighbors," he replied. "If you'd rather pay me a dollar for every bushel you pick, why I—"

She burst out laughing before he had finished the sentence. "You *do* put a high price on common wild laurel."

"So do you. I hear tell you call it green treasure," he said slyly.

She must somehow make him understand that she was willing to pay him all that she could afford to, but that his offers were out of the question. "Believe me, Mr. Libbey," she began earnestly, "my profits in this business are small. I call the laurel 'green treasure' because I am so glad to find some way of making extra money here at home, but—"

"I've made you two offers. Take them or leave them," he interrupted, smiling as if he had not believed a word she had been saying and rising from his chair.

Someone, she decided, had told him that she was getting rich selling Christmas greens, and nothing she could say would dislodge that idea from his brain.

"There's only one thing I *can* do—leave them."

"Good morning." He walked across the yard, climbed over the wall, then called back over his shoulder, "If you change your mind, let me know."

Janet knew from the way he loitered on the other side of the wall that he half expected to be called back.

"Take them or leave them!" she fumed to herself. "Just trying to accommodate a neighbor!" He was determined to force her into a partnership with him, a partnership in which he shared profits without expenses. He had been shrewd enough to see how anxious she was for laurel. Yes, she had read in his narrow eyes how sure he felt that he had only to name his terms. That promise that his children would pick for her had been part of the game he was playing to appear friendly and cooperative while driving a merciless bargain.

"What did that old hoss-trader want?" asked Etta when Janet came into the kitchen a little while later. In spite of putting her ear to the latch-hole, she had been able to catch only snatches of the conversation.

"He wanted to be neighborly."

"Humph! Don't believe it."

"By the way," the girl went on, ignoring Etta's curiosity, "have you any idea where Papa is? It's dinnertime, and he doesn't seem to be anywhere around."

"Land o' Goshen! Ain't he back yet? It was hours ago he started for the Center—right after you went up in the woods. Said he had to go to the store. Maybe Nancy cast a shoe."

Etta was glad she had cooked a boiled dinner—something easy to keep hot—for the old clock struck twelve, half past twelve, one, and half past one before there sounded from the yard the long "halloo-oo" Mr. Bradley always called out to announce his homecoming.

Chapter XXII

Just Like a Picnic

Janet saw in her father's eyes that little glint which always meant he was pleased about something. Well, it would be gone when he had heard about Mr. Libbey's neighborliness. She waited till he had finished two plates of corned beef and cabbage and a wide wedge of apple pie, washed down with plenty of hot tea. Then, having sent Etta to the workshop to rest her feet and help Mrs. Matthews, she reproduced the talk in the sitting room.

"He's got me just where he wants me, and he knows it," she lamented with tears of anger in her voice. "I'll either have to come to terms with him or write Reed Brothers I can't fill their order. And if I do that, I'll probably never get another order from them. Oh! It's terrible!"

The glint only brightened. "Oh no, he hasn't got you where he wants you, not by a jugful," said Mr. Bradley calmly. "I've been transacting a little business this morning myself. On the way to the Center, I stopped at the sawmill and had a little talk with Ned Warren. Then I drove to Bear Hill. There's oceans of laurel on that hill—enough to supply the whole of New England with Christmas greens, and last year Ned bought all that land."

"Really," thought Janet, "why couldn't Papa have more sense?" Then, out loud she asked, "What good is all that laurel to me or anybody else? Who's going to go traipsing off over there into the wilderness and get his eyes scratched out and his clothes torn to pieces picking the stuff and then carry it on his back for a couple of miles down the mountain?"

"Just hold your horses a minute until I get through talking. You don't even know what Bear Hill looks like now. There's a log road almost to the top and big cleared places where the laurel's thick as spatter and so easy to pick Molly could gather it. I know what I'm talking about, for I climbed the hill this morning and took a look for myself. Of course, the road is full of stumps and stones, but anybody with a little gumption can get through there with a heavy wagon and not have much trouble.

"Now, my idea is this," he went on before his daughter could ask any more questions. "We'll have laurel-picking bees every Saturday and take as many people as we can get into a hay wagon and still leave room for a big load of laurel. That is, we'll take them if they're willing to work hard all day. It will be a sort of working bee, picnic, and straw ride all in one. What do you think of that for a plan?"

He did not wait for her to answer. "You just couldn't guess what Ned has offered to do for us. He says his pair of workhorses just eat themselves pot-bellied this time of year when the farm work's about done and the winter logging hasn't begun yet. So we can have the use of them for nothing."

He stopped talking now and waited for his daughter to speak. The glint had become a twinkle.

Meantime, Janet's face had been a study in swiftly changing expressions. Pessimism had given way to just the merest shade of hopefulness, then to a look of genuine relief that erased the anxious wrinkle between her eyebrows.

"Oh, Papa, that's a great idea!" she exulted. "And won't it

be fun going on all-day trips like that. I can hardly wait to tell Delia and Roy. They've been so worried about those bicycles. The Matthews boys can pick now, and so can Billy Hastings. I'll ask Marie and Napoleon to come at least one Saturday even if they can pick at home; they'd love it so." She went on a run out through the woodshed to the shop to tell Etta and Mrs. Matthews the good news.

On the following Saturday, Janet cooked breakfast by lamplight. By the time the sun had come up, the dishes were done, a big basketful of lunch had been packed, and the two girls had put on their oldest shoes and stockings and everyday coats and caps. They were ready and waiting on the porch before their father, who was collecting the pickers, was halfway back up the hill with his load.

"Listen. They're coming. Oh, it *is* going to be like a straw ride," Molly cried. Up through the woods rang happy voices singing—

> "In a cavern, in a canyon,
> Excavating for a mine,
> Dwelt a miner, forty-niner,
> And his daughter, Clementine."

Into the yard trotted the two Warren horses hitched to a hay wagon. On a bed of straw in the bottom of the wagon were Mrs. Hastings and Etta, Mrs. Matthews, Emma, Sam and Jimmy, the two Millers, Napoleon and Marie Dubois, and to everyone's surprise, Mrs. Dubois and the baby. On the driver's seat with Mr. Bradley sat Billy Hastings. There was a wide grin on every face.

"There'll be a hot time in the old town tonight," struck up Billy as they started out again. Yes, it was like a straw ride and like a picnic, only more fun than either one, at least so Janet thought, and the others chattered and sang and laughed all the way to Bear Hill as if they were off for the biggest kind of lark. They kept up their merry talk while they clambered about on the hill among stumps and over boulders, filling their sacks with shiny green leaves. The crows and the hawks flew off cawing and screaming in dismay at having their privacy disturbed. A red fox retreated far into his den, wondering if the family in the valley had discovered that he was robbing their chicken roost. Panicky rabbits, who had never seen so many people before, made record-breaking hops as they scurried to their holes.

When the noonday sun lay warm on the hillside, the pickers selected a flat boulder as wide as a giant's dining table, spread a cloth upon it, and pooled the contents of baskets and pails. A game of Duck on the Rock followed, and then everybody went back to work again. Higher and higher rose the heap of laurel-filled sacks in the wagon. No one wanted to go home. Not till Mr. Bradley insisted that there wouldn't be room for the pickers to ride if any more sacks were dumped on the load would they stop work.

"Too bad somebody don't invent a way to make a picnic out of farm chores," declared Billy Hastings. "I guess I've worked harder today than I do at home even in haying time, but I didn't even know I was working, we was all talking and joshing so much."

"Can me and Napoleon come again next Saturday?" begged Marie. "It's heaps more fun than picking in our woods by ourselves."

"I don't see why not," Janet told them and was rewarded by two rapturous smiles.

Mrs. Matthews wanted to know if she couldn't bring Ben next week. "He's so skinny that he don't take up much room, and he'd have such a lovely time," she pleaded.

"Of course he can come, if you don't think he'll get too tired."

"I'll see that he don't. It'll do him good."

The laurel pickers were quieter on the way home than they had been on the outward trip. Molly and the two Matthews boys curled up on the straw, pillowed their heads on sacks of laurel, and were asleep before the horses had turned off the logging road. Mrs. Hastings and Mrs. Matthews were content to sit and say nothing. Etta hummed softly to herself. Janet leaned back and dreamily watched the clouds change shapes overhead. Roy and Delia were thoughtful. Marie and Napoleon chattered, but now they talked in French, for they could not do justice to the day in English. Liveliest of all was Billy. He sang as merrily now in the evening as he had at the break of day.

"He's like he used to be," his mother whispered to Janet.

The horses went slowly down the mountain road, held back by Mr. Bradley's firm hand on the reins, but when they came to the level stretch between Bear Hill and Laurel Hill, they trotted like colts, so eager were they to be home. It was all their driver could do to keep them from turning in at the Warren place instead of going on over the hill. From there they kept their ears laid back and would not stir faster than a poky walk.

At the Bradley house, everyone got out and helped unload the sacks of laurel. Then each claimed his own pickings, which were identified by a special mark, weighed his sacks on the scales in the workshop, and received his pay.

"Seems funny to get pay for having so much fun," said Billy.

Janet rode back to the Warrens' with her father when he returned the horses and wagon. Her heart was full of gratitude to Mr. Warren, and she wanted to tell him so herself.

"There's nothing to thank me for," he insisted. "That laurel is no use to me, and the horses don't have enough to do this time of year. Besides, I like to see a youngster doing the sort of thing you're doing, Janet, making the most of opportunities right here at home. Most boys and girls nowadays think that the first thing to do is to get off the farm." There was a wistful look in his face. "Janet, you keep right on with your little business on Laurel Hill."

"I'm a-going to. Nothing can stop me now." Then she asked the question she had wanted to ask the minute they drove into the yard. "When is Steve coming home?"

"Not till Thanksgiving. That's three weeks off, ain't it? He wrote his mother that he was too busy to come any sooner, but whether it's work or play that keeps him busy, I can't tell you."

She was silly to believe Stephen when he told her he'd be coming home often. He'd been in college more than a month now and hadn't spent a single weekend at home. She wondered soberly if he would seem different when she saw him again.

Chapter XXIII

The Hill's Afire

It was only by chance that Janet went to the woods that November afternoon. She was working on pine wreaths and ran short of pine. Br-r-r! She shivered as she started out against the cold wind. Afterward, it made her shiver to think what might have happened if she had stayed by the fire.

The outlines of the pines were blurred, and the spaces between them filled with a blue haze. The haze grew thicker and thicker. Yet Janet did not notice these things. Her eyes were on the ground as she pulled long green streamers from the needles and moss. She stood up. Why, the woods were full of smoke! It was drifting down over the top of the hill. How many rabbits and squirrels there were about! They were all scurrying in the same direction—down the hill.

Up over the slippery needles among the brown tree trunks she ran, over the wall and down through the woods on the other side. The smoke grew thicker. At the edge of the clearing, she stopped. Halfway down the hill, a cloud of flame-illumined smoke rose above the bushes and grass. The girl cried out as if she herself had been burned. The wind was blowing those flames nearer and nearer to the woods, and if these trees caught fire, no one could save her own woods—her green treasure.

Now she was running again—this time in the same direction as the rabbits and squirrels. Back to the wall and over it, out of the woods, into the upper lot she sped, not pausing once to get her breath or when her legs began to ache. Every second counted now. In such a wind, even these fields, even their house, might be in danger.

In the middle lot, she began to shout, "Help! Help! Fire! Fire! Papa, come quick!"

Mr. Bradley was out of the barn in a moment. From the woodshed door popped Billy Hastings like a puppet pulled by a string. Mrs. Matthews and Mrs. Hastings and Etta trooped into the yard after him. All four began to peer about—up at the chimney and roof of the house, then at the barn, expecting to see flames appear at any moment. There was no fire. What was the matter with the girl?

"The hill! The hill's afire!" she shouted, waving her arm back toward the dark treetops. By this time, wisps of blue smoke could be seen drifting above them.

Mr. Bradley dashed into the barn and came out with shovels, axes, and pitchforks. "Come on, Billy," he called, dividing the tools with him. "Etta, go to the Warrens and the Clarks and tell them Laurel Hill's afire. Here, don't go like that. Put your hat and coat on."

Never before in her life had Janet felt so much as if she were living a terrible dream as during the next few hours. The events of that afternoon and evening were blurred and disconnected as in a dream. Afterward, she never could give a clear account of just what happened from the time she gave the alarm till, aching from head to foot, she crawled into bed.

She did not remember going back over the hill, but she recalled being in the Libbey pasture with an old broom in her hands, beating, beating, beating, beating at tongues of flame that disappeared in one spot only to dart out in another.

Around her, others were beating as desperately as she was. Yet the fire kept coming on, on.

Photographed in her mind was a small juniper bush as the flames shot through it, turning every lacy twig incandescent. It was so beautiful and so terrible to see. Janet pictured the giant pines in the Christmas woods glowing beautiful like that, then only black stumps. Could they stop those flames before it was too late?

She saw how the perspiration dripped from the faces of the men who were digging in frantic haste, laying bare a wide strip of earth. Could they make it wide enough in the time left to them? Or would the wind blow the fire right across it up to the woods and on—and on? How small her father and the others looked against the background of tall trees. And the voice of the wind was louder than their voices.

Now a loose-jointed boy came up the hill from the house below, grinning delightedly at the sight that met his eyes. It was the Libbey boy. In the excitement, no one had thought of routing out the Libbeys to fight their own fire. Recognizing Janet, he came up to her and announced proudly, "I done it."

She looked at him with horror. "Don't you know that the whole hill, all the woods, even our house, even yours if the wind changes, may burn up? Here, take this broom and beat for all you're worth, and for mercy sakes, stop grinning."

To her surprise, he took the broom and went soberly to work. Childish terror was in his face now. "I didn't suppose nothing would burn but the grass," he said, half-whimpering.

"Where's your Pa? He ought to be here too."

"He ain't home. Ain't nobody home but me."

A few minutes later, an angry voice was heard even above the wind and the crackling flames. "I'll have you arrested, all of you, if you don't tell me who done this." Jack Libbey, back from the Center, was in their midst, sure that plotting neighbors had taken advantage of his absence to set his pasture afire.

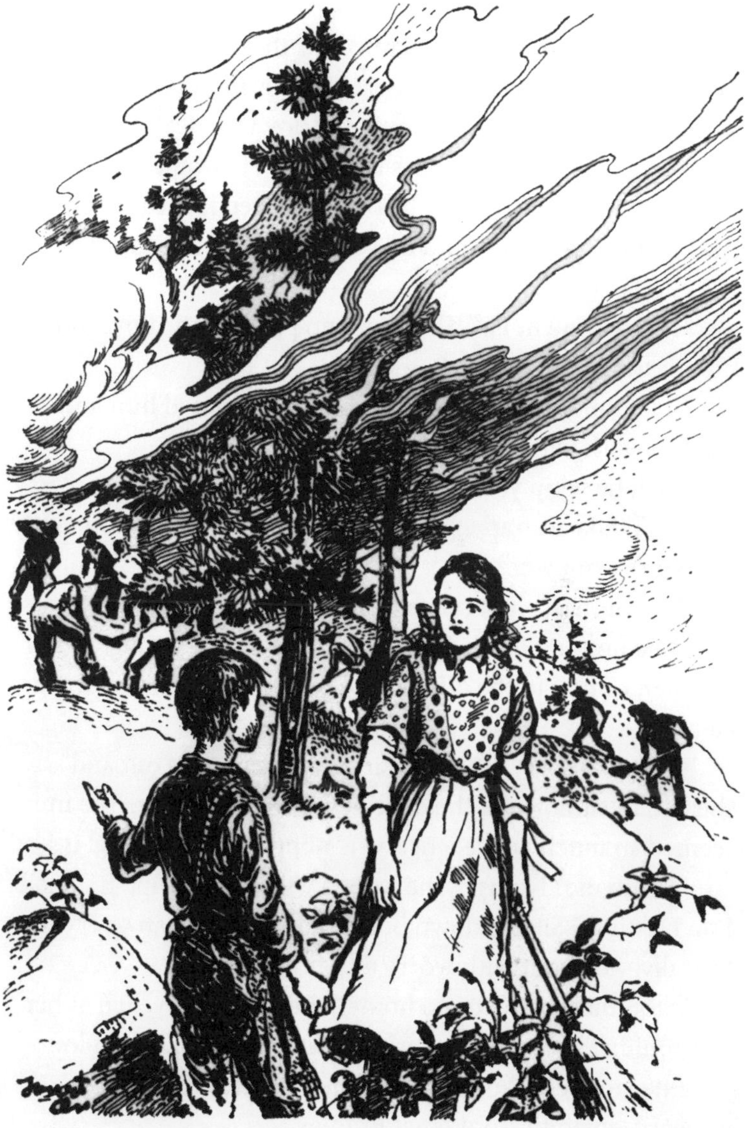

The men went on working and paid no attention to the angry man. There was no time to argue now.

"I'll bet I know who done it. It was that laurel-picking gal, that Bradley gal."

So she was going to be blamed for this! She who had discovered it and had nearly beaten her arms loose from their sockets trying to help put it out. The boy was stealing terror-stricken glances in his father's direction. He would never confess, and she would not be believed even if she told on him. And that mean man would do something terrible to get square with her.

"I—I—done it, Pa." There was no pride in the boy's voice now. It trembled.

Jack Libbey took the shovel someone handed him and went to work without another word.

"Will he whip you?" Janet asked the boy beside her.

"He'll take a strap to me sure, but," he added triumphantly, "he won't whip *you*."

The funniest sight that afternoon was Grandpa Matthews. He came limping down from the spring with a small pail full of water, calling to the others, "I'll put it out. Been fighting fires all my life."

Janet was sorry when her arms and legs gave out and she had to sit down at the edge of the woods to rest. The fire seemed so much worse when you stopped and watched it.

"It's no use! No use! The woods will all burn up," moaned Etta Hastings. Sitting down beside Janet, she began to cry hysterically, worn out with worry and firefighting.

"Stop that crying or go home," the other girl yelled at her. She couldn't bear to hear her own thoughts spoken out loud.

Etta stopped, shocked out of her hysterics by such unheard-of wrath from Janet Bradley.

How long she sat on the hillside feeling her face grow hotter and hotter and yet shivering, Janet never knew. She lost count of the number of times she retreated as the heat increased. Her father wanted her to go home, but she could not bring herself to leave. It would be worse to sit at home watching the sky for flames to burst over the pointed tops of those trees.

To keep her mind off even worse calamities, she began gloomily to think of the animals that would lose their homes in the woods—the wood thrush that nested every year in the old oak above the spring; the ovenbird whose nest she could never find, though she knew it was on the ground, either under the oak or under the hemlock beside it; the red squirrel in the hollow beech near the wall. Her lower lip quivered, and she held it tight with her upper teeth. If she didn't look out, she'd be going to pieces like Etta.

Through her despair, a voice broke. It was her father's. "Thank goodness! What a blessing from God! The wind's going down with the sun," he cried.

The girl was glad it was dusky now at the edge of the woods. Her father's words seemed to loosen the hold she had on her lower lip, and when her lips began to tremble, tears of relief started down her cheeks. She checked them quickly before anyone could discover how unstrung she was.

Yes, the wind was dying down. With every minute, the woods grew quieter. "Thank you, God! Thank you, God!" she said over and over to herself. The men could fight back the flames from the woods now.

Going home over the hill, she put her hands out and touched the tree trunks lovingly as she passed them. Those tall brown columns still stood reaching up to the sky.

The kitchen windows were yellow squares of light. Oh dear! Was Molly trying to cook supper alone? How much there would be to do at home! She hadn't thought about Molly or supper or the cows waiting to be milked. The humming of the cream separator greeted her ears, and sounds of dishes clinking and stove covers rattling came from the kitchen.

"Why, Mrs. Matthews!" she exclaimed at the sight of that lady turning the separator crank. "I thought you went home."

"I did so, but I come back again when I'd cooked supper for my family."

"But who did the milking?"

"I did, and not the first time I've milked a cow either."

Janet sniffed when she opened the kitchen door. She recognized two distinct smells. One came from the big company coffee pot on the stove. The other was—yes, it was—the smell of biscuits baking. On the table a large boiled ham reposed, waiting to be sliced and oozing juices onto a platter—a ham that had not come from the Bradley pantry. Mrs. Hastings, Etta, and Molly bustled about.

The girl stood with her mouth open wide. She hadn't even seen Etta or Mrs. Hastings leave the pasture.

"It's just too good to be true—cows milked, cream separated, supper cooked—and I thought all those things still had to be done. But where in the world did that ham come from?"

"Now, wasn't it lucky I boiled a big ham this morning? Something seemed to tell me to do it," said Mrs. Hastings. "Them men are going to be as hungry as hound dogs."

Janet and Etta and Mrs. Hastings went back over the hill together by lantern light, carrying baskets of rolls and sliced ham and pails of hot coffee to the men who would be beating out flames and embers for hours longer. In one basket, Janet tucked an enormous wedge of mince pie and a slice of applesauce cake. "Perhaps," she told the Libbey boy when she put the pie in one of his hands and the cake in the other, "this will help you not mind that whipping so much. You were a brick to fess up and not let your father think I started the fire."

The boy took an enormous bite of pie and said, with his

mouth oozing crumbs and filling, "I'd take a licking every day for pie like this here."

Jack Libbey looked sheepish when Janet offered him refreshments.

"You folks saved my woods," he said, "and after this, if you want to pick laurel here, you can."

The girl's face wore a grim smile in the lantern light. She glanced down at the hillside, where the smoke still rose from the grass and bushes.

"I'm afraid, Mr. Libbey, that offer comes a little late."

For weeks after that night, Janet felt grateful every time she looked up the hill at the pines against the sky. Her green treasure was safe!

Soon after the fire, the "Keep Off" signs vanished from the other side of the wall.

Chapter XXIV

Janet Regrets

It was the day after Thanksgiving. The long table in the woodshed workroom was covered with laurel and ground pine. The air was laden with the piney fragrance of the woods. Women and girls talked happily while their fingers moved swiftly among the heaps of green treasure. Boys and men moved in and out, carrying sacks on their backs and rolling out barrels packed full of green ropes and wreaths. Mrs. Matthews and Emma were there and Mrs. Hastings and Etta, who had been called out of the kitchen to help during these last hurried days. So were Delia and Mary and Marie Dubois. Napoleon Dubois and Sam Matthews were unloading a wagonful of laurel at the woodshed door. And within the shed, Mr. Matthews and Billy Hastings nailed on barrelheads and painted them in large black letters with the name, Moore & Smollet, and the address.

Janet was everywhere. Red spots burned in her cheeks as she hurried about, inspecting the finished work of her helpers at the table, counting wreaths and measuring lengths of roping, making entries in her black book, paying off laurel pickers, and going to the kitchen to answer a call of distress from Molly, who was valiantly struggling with preparations for dinner.

Two weeks remained before the last barrel must be taken to the railroad station—two hectic weeks. Compared with this season, last year's rush to fill orders had been leisurely. Yet how Janet loved all this hurrying and scurrying indoors and out, the sense of having set all this activity in motion.

> *"Oh, Lord Jeffrey Amherst was a soldier of the king,*
> *And he came from across the sea,*
> *To the Frenchmen and the Indians he didn't do a thing*
> *In the wilds of this wild country."*

The girl looked up quickly from the pile of wreaths she was counting to see Stephen lounging in the doorway. My, but he had grown taller already, and wasn't he good-looking in that white turtleneck sweater and that purple-banded hat cocked on one side of his head? "Want some help?" he asked, with no expectation that the offer would be taken seriously. He took off his hat with a flourish, as if he wanted everyone to notice its purple band.

"Hello, Steve. Sure, I want help. You can count these wreaths while I go and see what Molly wants now."

"Say, look here! I didn't come to work. I want to talk to you." He picked his way swaggeringly across the littered floor.

"I'll be back in just a minute."

"Oh dear!" Janet said to herself. "He's changed—in two months. I can see it. He's changed into a smarty and a show-off."

It took more than a minute to straighten things out in the kitchen, where Molly wept over the charred remains of a cottage pudding she had baked for dinner. By the time the girl had been calmed and set to work making a boiled custard, Mr. Bradley was calling from the woodshed to ask whether Napoleon and Sam should pick any more laurel. To answer his question, Janet had to make a trip to the barn and count the bags stored there. Twenty minutes had passed before she was back in the workshop, though it seemed to her no more than three or four.

Stephen was doing a cakewalk up and down the room with a laurel wreath around his neck and, at the same time, was trying to lasso Delia with a long loop of laurel. Work at the table was at a standstill. "Rubberneck," he called to Janet, who looked at him as if he were a small boy in need of a spanking.

"Don't Steve. You'll tear that all to pieces. Put it back in the barrel, please. Did you count those wreaths on the floor?" She tried to keep her voice even and pleasant-sounding, but it had a knife-like edge without her realizing it.

The boy tilted his head back and looked down his shapely nose at her, just as if he were acting in a play, Janet thought. "Sa-ay, who was your waiter last year?" The scornful voice did not sound like Stephen at all.

"Come on into the house where we can talk," she said quickly. "Mary, will you count those and write the number down in my book and then tell Papa he can pack them?"

"So nice of you to spare me a moment of your valuable time, Miss Bradley," the boy went on in the same sarcastic voice when they had pulled up chairs close to the sitting-room stove.

"Oh, Steve, I'm sorry I had to keep you waiting. I'm awfully glad to see you, really. Now, tell me all about college."

Stephen's nose dropped immediately to its normal attitude. "It can't be beat. And just wait until you hear about my surprise. The musical clubs are giving a concert two weeks from tonight in Northbrook, and yours truly is going to be—*on the platform singing in the Glee Club*. What do you think of that?"

"You've made the Glee Club already? My, but I *am* proud of you!"

"That isn't all I've got to tell you. I want you to come and hear me sing at my first big concert. Ma and Pa are going to drive up, and you can go with them."

"Oh, Steve, I'd give anything to go, but I can't possibly. You see—"

"You can't?" The boy sounded the way a king might if one of his subjects had refused an invitation to a royal fete.

"I'll probably have to work till midnight that night. The middle of December is the busiest time in the whole year for me. If only the concert came earlier or later, I'd jump at the chance to go."

"If Prexy Harris knew how busy you are just now, he'd probably change the college calendar. Honestly, Janet, anybody'd think to hear you that there wasn't a thing in the world so important as that Christmas-greens business of yours."

"And anybody'd think to hear *you* go on, Steve Warren, that the sun rose and set right on that college campus, while the rest of us sat in outer darkness and did nothing of any consequence." She sounded downright spiteful now, and she knew it and didn't care if she did.

The boy snatched at his hat as if it might burn up if he left it a moment longer on the davenport, clapped it on his head at an even more rakish angle than before, and jerked the door open. "There are plenty of girls that will jump at the chance to go to that concert, *even Smith College girls*," he called over his shoulder without looking at her. The heavy door shut behind him with a slam that made the windows rattle.

"Go off mad! See if I care!" she cried out defiantly to the empty room, then burst into tears and ran upstairs to her chamber and threw herself face down on the bed.

Never before in all the years had she and Steve quarreled like this. How maddening he had been with his airs and his patronizing manner! Why couldn't he understand that her work was as important to her as college was to him? And that parting shot! "Even Smith College girls!" As if they were superior beings. That was the meanest thing he had ever said.

The spot on the old patchwork quilt where her face rested grew damper and damper.

Meanwhile, Stephen, striding down the hill as if he were catching a train, scowled and talked out loud to himself. "She acts as if an invitation to a concert of the Amherst Musical Clubs was nothing at all, nothing at all. I suppose the skies would fall if she didn't get those plaguey wreaths and things done. Well, just see if I ever ask her to go anywhere again—not if she crawls down Laurel Hill on her knees and begs me to."

"Janet! Janet!" called Molly from the kitchen.

"Where are you, Janet?" It was her father calling now.

The girl jumped up, bathed her eyes in the bowl on the washstand, and looked at herself carefully in the glass. Then she reappeared in the workshop, her face expressionless. With feverish haste, she began to weigh bags of laurel on the scales that stood in the corner of the shop.

"You've weighed those before," Mrs. Hastings reminded her, but she had to repeat the information three times before the girl heard her.

The more she thought about the matter, the worse it seemed to have quarreled with the best friend she had in the world. He was enough to make a saint mad. Still and all, perhaps she had not been as nice to him as she should have been, when he offered her such a treat. Well, she would see him when he came home for Christmas vacation and try to make him understand that she really had appreciated the invitation.

Janet saw Stephen the Sunday before Christmas, but Stephen did not see her. That is, he looked steadily in the opposite direction whenever she was within his range of vision and carefully avoided being within speaking distance of her. When she came out of church, Ethel Hayes stood on the steps surrounded by a group of listening girls. "It was just thrilling," she was telling them, "and after the concert, we had supper at the Brook House, and—"

So Ethel was the Smith girl who had "jumped at the chance" to go to the concert. They were birds of a feather all right—those two. Ethel gave herself as many airs over going to college this fall as Steve did.

Janet did not wait to hear the rest of that sentence. She did not stop to talk with any of the girls and boys or wait for her father to untie Nancy and drive around to the horse block. Instead, she followed him out to the sheds at the back of the church and sat in the buggy while he swapped talk with the other men.

"Well, you *are* in a hurry to go home," he told her.

"My stomach feels funny," she said.

Chapter XXV

Janet is Eighteen

"Are you sure that clock is right? It seems lots later than four o'clock."

"Mamma set it by the noon whistle," Delia Miller answered truthfully, but she failed to add that she had pushed the hands back exactly one hour just before Janet arrived. "Come on, let's coast down to the bridge again. You're getting so you can ride a bike just as well as Roy and I."

"All right. One more ride. Then I must go home."

Off went the two girls. Delia, wearing a divided skirt, straddled the bar of her brother's bicycle while Janet rode Delia's. *Cling! Cling! Cling!* rang the bells on the handlebars. Bicycle riding was still a fascinating novelty to the Millers, though they had possessed the coveted new chainless machines since April. Now that Delia had learned to ride, she was teaching Janet, because, as she and Roy put it, "We wouldn't have had any bicycles for at least another year if you hadn't hired us to help you last fall."

"You hardly wobbled at all that time. Why don't we go as far as the schoolhouse?"

Janet was firm. She had to go home and start supper.

As they pushed their bicycles back up the road toward the

Millers', Delia suddenly began to limp. "Got to rest my ankle," she explained, sitting down on a fallen tree trunk by the road. "Guess I twisted it. Wait just a minute, and I'll be all right. Then I'll walk up to the woods with you."

The minute lengthened to ten minutes while Janet fidgeted. The girl on the log watched her out of the corner of her eyes, as if trying to estimate how long the other's patience would hold out.

"You're limping on the other foot now," remarked Janet when they walked on again.

Delia flushed. "Well, er, both my ankles seem to hurt."

It seemed as if Delia had never been so slow in her life or found so many reasons for dawdling along the way. She tied her shoe. She stopped to pick black-eyed Susans. She just had to have a drink at the spring in the Hastings' pasture and took a long time getting it. At the edge of the woods, she suddenly decided to go on to the next ridge.

"It's a grand long coast down from there," she explained.

Janet said nothing out loud, but to herself, "At this rate, it will be another twenty minutes before I'm home, and I wanted to frost that cake and bake biscuits for supper. Ought to celebrate my eighteenth birthday somehow. Nobody else seems even to remember it *is* my birthday."

She was eighteen years old today—a young lady. And apparently neither Molly nor her father nor Delia nor anyone she knew remembered what day it was—the tenth of July. For years Mary Clark had given her a birthday present. Stephen had never forgotten this day before. Of course, she didn't expect Stephen even to come and see her now. He had been as stiff as a poker ever since that time last November when she had refused his invitation to the concert. He never could seem to understand that she really had to stay at home then or lose out in her business. It was terrible for her and Steve—of all people—to quarrel and to drift farther and farther apart.

"I've just got to hurry on," she told Delia firmly when the latter sat down again to rest. To her surprise, Delia jumped up, got onto her bicycle, and, instead of turning back, went pedaling up the slope to the Bradley house, calling saucily over her shoulder, "I'll beat you home."

"She acts crazy as all get out today," thought Janet.

In spite of her haste to be home, the girl stopped for an instant at the beginning of the avenue of maples. The house at the end of those rows of trees was not dark and forbidding now, but white as the clouds that floated above the roof. She couldn't get used to seeing the house like this, though it was more than two months since Ed Cowing and Papa had given it that spotless coat of paint. How friendly and welcoming it seemed!

Just as she stepped onto the porch, Janet heard whispers, then a giggle. Was that Mary? It sounded like her. Someone said, "Sh-h-h! She's coming!" That was Roy Miller's voice.

> *"Happy birthday to you!*
> *Happy birthday to you!"*

Singing voices floated through the screen door. Janet stood still in amazement. "It's a surprise party," called Molly. "There's a cake with—" A firm hand clapped over the child's mouth, prevented her from giving away any more information about the delights to come.

The sitting room was full of people—Mary and Delia and Roy; Etta and Billy; the three oldest Matthews children; Marie and Napoleon Dubois; and Miss Evans, the Roaring Brook School teacher, who had been tutoring Janet for nearly a year. From the kitchen came the voices of Mrs. Clark, Mrs. Miller, Mrs. Matthews, and Mrs. Hastings, who, judging from the sounds and smells, were preparing an elaborate supper.

"Many happy returns, Janet," they called from the doorway. "Don't come out here if you know what's good for you," warned Mrs. Miller.

"Set one foot over this threshold, and I'll give you eighteen of the hardest spanks a girl ever had on her birthday," added Mrs. Clark.

"If I'm having a party, I'm going to dress up for it," announced Janet. When every guest had had a chance to kiss her or wish her, shyly, many happy returns, she ran upstairs and took down from the closet her Sunday best dress of white muslin and began unbuttoning the checked gingham she had worn to Delia's.

The fragrances of food now overflowed the kitchen and even floated upstairs. In a few minutes, Mrs. Clark was calling, "Supper's ready when you're ready, Janet."

"Coming!" Janet struggled to finish buttoning the last small pearl buttons between her shoulder blades, pulled out the short curls about her ears, put on her bracelets, gave a last look at herself in the mirror, and rejoined her impatient guests—or rather, hosts and hostesses—below. Roy Miller rose ceremoniously and offered his arm, then led her through the kitchen, the back kitchen, out into the woodshed, and up the steps to the workshop. The others trooped after them.

In the doorway, the girl stood still. "Oh, how beautiful! How beautiful!" she cried. The room had been transformed into an evergreen woods, or something as near like it as a room could be. Ropes of laurel were festooned from the hanging lamp over the table to the sides of the room. Sprays of ground pine were twined around the window frames. Small evergreen trees stood in the corners of the room. At every place was a sprig of pine. In two silver candlesticks lent by Mrs. Clark were tall red candles. A looking glass laid flat on the table, and bordered with green moss and ferns, was like a clear pool of water.

Not until she was seated between Roy Miller and Billy Hastings, with Mrs. Clark beaming at her from one end of the table and her father from the other, could Janet stop looking and begin to talk. "It's as lovely as my green woods, and you've even brought a spring into the house," she added, pointing to the looking glass. "Now I understand why Delia was so slow this afternoon and seemed set on keeping me from getting home. You've all been working hard, but I guess she worked fully as hard as any of you."

It was fun to sit back and let other people bring in food they had cooked in her kitchen. The "piece of resistance," as Molly called it, in imitation of Roy's French, was, of course, the birthday cake—a mound of whiteness surrounded by a garland of laurel and topped with eighteen red candles. The tiny flames brought a radiance into the room. One of them was reflected in each of Janet's eyes when she leaned over and let her breath out with a *pouf*.

Molly, who took this ceremony with great seriousness, watched anxiously and looked enormously relieved when four flames burned on after her sister had blown. Thank goodness! Janet wasn't going to get married for four years. By that time, she herself would be almost grown up—fourteen years old!

When everyone had eaten at least two slices of cake and a small pyramid of the ice cream brought by Mrs. Clark in her White Mountain freezer, when favors had been popped and cheery caps put on, Billy Hastings rose and rapped the table loudly with the handle of his pocket knife. Clearing his throat nervously and pulling at his collar as if it were about to close in on his windpipe, he began in a platform voice, "Ladies and gentlemen, I don't know why I'm the one elected to make a speech tonight, but—"

"Because this party was your idea in the first place," interrupted Roy.

"Well, I did kinder get the ball a-rolling," went on Billy in his natural voice, "but everybody here except Janet pushed the ball along. Anyway, Janet, to make a long story short, we folks that worked for you last winter wanted to show what we thought of you, and we decided to celebrate this day and to—er—" He fumbled in first one pocket then another and finally pulled out a small package. "Here's a little birthday present for you," he added quickly, then dropped into his chair, explaining in a stage whisper to Delia, who sat beside him, "I had a fine speech all learned by heart and just as soon as I got up, I forgot every word of it."

The package was wrapped in white tissue paper and tied with red and green ribbons like a Christmas present. There was silence the length of the table while the guest of honor unwrapped the parcel and opened the cardboard box. On a bed of black velvet lay the prettiest watch she had ever seen—a chatelaine watch—the latest style. Janet lifted it up as if she thought the very touch of her fingers might break it.

Delia rose from her place beside Billy and fastened the watch to Janet's dress just below the left shoulder. Then Billy was on his feet again, having recalled some of the things he had forgotten to say. He pointed to the leafy design engraved around the face of the watch and the spray of the leaves that formed the pin. "I don't know whether them are intended for laurel leaves or not, but that's what the ladies that picked this watch out say they are. Anyhow, we thought 'twas kind of appropriate to have leaves on it, because everybody that worked on your Christmas greens contributed to this gift. Of course, we had to let in a few outsiders that we knew you'd want to have invited—Miss Clark and Miss Miller and the schoolteacher."

Now the girl was standing up, thanking everybody for the supper and for the watch and for all the help they had given her in the past.

At this point, the party threatened to turn into an experience meeting. Roy Miller felt moved to tell the company that he and Delia wouldn't have got their bicycles this spring if it hadn't been for the money they'd made last fall working for

Janet. Mrs. Matthews said that if Janet's birthday had come a few weeks later, Ben could have been there. He could walk a little already, and it was the money she and the children earned last fall, added to what Emma made cleaning house for folks at the Center and a little they had saved before, that had paid for the operation on his hip. She'd be grateful to Janet all the days of her life.

"Where's Steve Warren?" asked Mrs. Hastings suddenly, looking around as if she couldn't quite believe that the missing boy wasn't hiding under the table or behind the door. "Didn't you invite him, Billy?"

"Sure I did, but he couldn't come."

Janet kept her head bent low over her plate for a few moments.

"I've brought my new mandolin. Let's sing something," proposed Mary Clark quickly. She ran into the house and came back strumming and singing, "The sun shines bright in the old Kentucky home." One by one, the voices joined in the song. Other old-time favorites followed. When Mary produced the sheet music of a new ragtime tune, the boys and girls clustered eagerly around her to learn it. Soon all of them were singing—

> *"If you lak-a-me*
> *Lak I lak-a-you*
> *And we lak-a-both the same ..."*

"Janet, you aren't to do a thing," protested Mrs. Hastings. "You won't ever have an eighteenth birthday again." A general scraping and stacking of plates had begun. The girl thought she would carry at least one tray full of dishes to the kitchen, but wished afterwards she hadn't.

Just as she was about to push open the woodshed door, a low-voiced conversation came to her ears—a conversation that she would have given anything to have missed.

"Ma," Etta Hastings was saying, "what did you want to ask about Steve for? Didn't you know he and Janet were cool as cucumbers to each other, and that he was beauing Ethel Hayes around? He took her buggy riding somewhere tonight."

"For mercy sakes! I didn't have no idea those two had fallen out, and Billy didn't either."

"Some folks keep their eyes and ears tight shut." Etta's voice was scornful.

The listening girl waited till the two had passed on into the kitchen. When she pushed open the door, her head was high and her face utterly expressionless.

There were games and more songs before the guests said goodnight. Janet stood on the porch for a few minutes after the last one had left, watching the moving paths of light made by the lanterns and listening to the voices. She was strangely subdued for a girl who had just been given a surprise party.

> *"If you lak-a-me*
> *Lak I lak-a-you*
> *And we lak-a-both the same …"*

floated back up the road.

"I hate that new song," she thought, and she wished the whip-poor-will would stop singing in the backyard. He sounded so dismal.

The bird gave an abrupt "whip" and flew away. He had heard what the girl could not hear till several seconds later—hoofs beating in double-quick time on the road.

"Why, it's the doctor's Bess," cried Janet. "Somebody must be terribly sick."

Mr. Bradley stopped in the midst of winding the clock and rushed to the door. "Yes, that's the doctor all right. Haven't heard Bess tear by like that since the night Jim Hastings died."

Chapter XXVI

Stephen Loses His Memory

When Janet awoke next morning, almost her first thought was of Bess racing through the night. Her father, the moment he had finished breakfast, announced that he was going down to see if the Warrens knew who was sick.

"I hope Grandpa Matthews hasn't had a stroke or anything," he said.

Scarcely were the words spoken when the old man walked into the yard. "Have you heard about the Warren boy?" he panted.

Every trace of color went out of Janet's face. "What about him? What's happened?" The tight-throated voice did not sound like her own.

"I always said he'd break his neck with that skittish horse of his. She ain't safe to drive, and with these autos whizzing around and scaring horses to death, I don't know as anybody's safe—even driving an old plug."

"What about Steve?" broke in Janet.

The old man was now so well started on the subject of his favorite abomination that he did not even hear her question. "I tell you, Jim Bradley, those infernal machines ought not to be allowed on the public highways. If folks want to go tearing over the ground like that, they ought to make roads of their own, just like the railroads do."

"Look here, Gramp," said Mr. Bradley in a loud, firm voice, "never mind about automobiles for a minute. Tell us how bad off the Warren boy is."

"All I can tell you is that he and the Hayes girl was out buggy riding last night when one of them tarnal machines come along, and the horse run and took a wheel off the buggy, and he was thrown out and hit his head on a rock, and they picked him up unconscious and—"

Before the old man had finished his sentence, Janet was out of the yard. "I'm going right down to the Warrens' myself," she called to her father over her shoulder.

"Oh please, God, make him get well!" she prayed over and over.

From the Bradleys' house to the Warrens' was less than a quarter of a mile, but to Janet that morning, it seemed more like a mile, though she covered the distance in a shorter time than ever before. People who are drowning, she had heard, reviewed their whole lives in a moment or two. So, in the space of seven or eight minutes, she thought of all the pleasant things she and Stephen had done together, how they used to walk back and forth to the Roaring Brook School, then drove together to grammar school and later to the trains when they were in high school. Steve had helped her "find the value of x" in those bothersome algebra problems that had nearly reduced her to tears. At Sunday School picnics, he always took her out rowing, and on such occasions as chicken-pie suppers, he always sat beside her at the table. For those first few awful days after her mother died, she and Molly had stayed at the Warrens', and Steve, though he had never lost his mother or anybody he loved, seemed to understand just how she felt.

Grandma Warren answered the girl's knock. "He's bad. He don't even know his own mother," was her doleful reply to

Janet's inquiry. They sat down in the sitting room together and rocked back and forth, back and forth, in rocking chairs. "It's a mercy he wasn't killed. And yet, if he ain't going to be in his right mind—" The old lady finished the sentence by shaking her head grimly.

For a moment the visitor could not speak. She told herself that Grandma Warren always looked on the dark side of things. She was worse than Gramp Matthews about that. Yet suppose—suppose the old lady was right this time?

"What does the doctor say?" Janet asked.

"He says Steve'll come out of it all right. I hope he knows what he's talking about. Of course, he won't be able to walk for weeks. His ankle's broke."

The door into the downstairs bedroom opened, and Mrs. Warren entered the room. "I thought I heard your voice, Janet, and I'm so glad you've come," she exclaimed with evident relief. "Steve's rousing up a little, and he seems to be terribly worried about you."

"Me?"

"Yes, he kept muttering your name, and finally I made out that he thought you were hurt. He's all in a muddle, and I guess he's got it into his mind that you were out with him last night. Won't you stay awhile? I couldn't make him understand a thing. If you're here and he can see you next time he comes to, it might quiet him and help him to get well."

"Of course I'll stay," said Janet, "only I'll have to slip up home for a minute and tell Papa and Molly not to expect me till they see me."

"It's mighty fine of you to do this," Mrs. Warren told her when the girl was back, "for I know you and Steve haven't been 'hitting it off' lately, and I'm sorry about it, too." Before Janet could reply, she had gone back to the sickroom.

"Come quick," she called from the bedroom doorway a few minutes later.

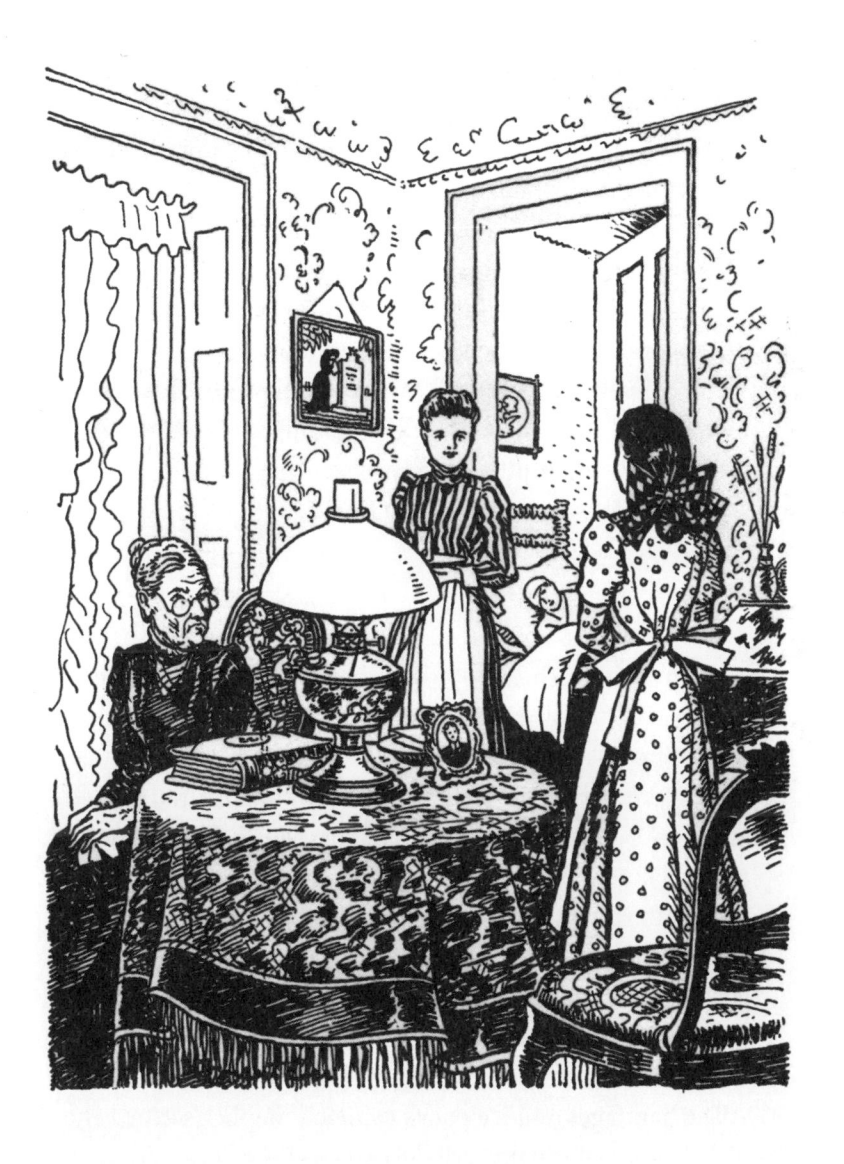

It was hard to recognize the figure on the bed as Stephen, or even as a person at all. His head and half his face were swathed in bandages. There was a puzzled, worried expression in his one visible blue eye.

"I'm all right, Steve, perfectly all right," said Janet, "not even scratched or bruised."

"It—it—wasn't—Fan's—fault." The words came slowly, as if each one had to be pulled up out of a deep well.

"I know, Steve, and it wasn't your fault either."

At these words, the eyes closed and the boy's head settled deep into the pillow, as if there were nothing more for him to worry about. Janet tiptoed out of the room.

"He's much quieter now," Mrs. Warren reported when she and Janet and Mr. Warren sat down to dinner. "He's stopped that moaning and muttering to himself."

Janet went home on skipping feet.

> *"If you lak-a-me*
> *Lak I lak-a-you"*

she began to sing, then stopped abruptly. How was Stephen going to act after his memory came back? That might happen any time now—and suddenly.

Next day, when she went to see him, she tortured herself all the way between the two houses. Perhaps he would be completely changed. Perhaps that one eye would stare at her coldly. Yet that afternoon, the boy grinned at her, once more like the old Stephen.

Day after day, Janet went through the same dread of being greeted in the distant "Oh-yes-I've-met-you-before-somewhere" manner of the days before the accident.

The bandages and ice packs came off Stephen's head. The purple bruises gradually faded to green and yellow. His memory of other things came back. Yet still he seemed to have forgotten that he and Janet had ever quarreled and that another girl had been his companion the night of the unlucky ride.

Then one day he gave a chuckle, looked straight into her eyes, and said, "Janet, you sure ought to go onto the stage. You're a regular actress."

"What do you mean?" she asked nervously.

"As a matter of fact," he went on without answering her question, "I've been acting too, for over a week. Just at first I *was* batty. Then, when everything came back to me, I decided that if you could pretend, I could too, that if you were willing to forget I stayed away from your birthday party and took Ethel out riding that same night just to be spiteful, I could forget that I was ever mad as a hornet at you. What do you say? Shall we keep right on forgetting?"

"I have already," said Janet. "It seems almost as if we *did* take that ride together and that I bumped *my* head, too."

They both laughed as if someone had told an excruciatingly funny joke, and Stephen said, growing serious, that he "guessed the accident had knocked a lot of nonsense out of his head." After that, they laughed some more just for the fun of laughing together.

What talks the boy and girl did have in the days that followed! And how much there was to tell each other. "Anybody'd think you two had been separated for years—the way you run on," Mrs. Warren exclaimed one day, beaming on both of them. Well, she knew that these long talks were good medicine for a boy who had to stay in bed while a broken bone was mending.

Every afternoon that she could, Janet came in to sit for a while with Stephen. Sometimes she brought her sewing bag. A pink chambray dress for Molly was basted up, and a shadow embroidery front for a blouse for herself was finished in the sickroom.

When the boy was able to lie upon the couch on the porch, the afternoons grew positively hilarious. He learned to plink-plink accompaniments on the new banjo his father bought for him, while he and Janet sang. Mary Clark came with her mandolin and sheet music of the latest ragtime songs. Delia and Roy pedaled into the yard, ringing their bicycle bells in a merry salute to the patient. The occasional passersby on the hill road would rein in their horses and stop to listen to young voices singing.

The doctor, arriving in the midst of one of these afternoon concerts, chuckled delightedly. "Well, for a young man who did his best to get killed, I must say you've made great progress. I don't care much for these new songs myself, but maybe I'll have to begin prescribing them for my patients—or is it the company that's doing you so much good?"

"The company," answered Stephen, looking at Janet.

Chapter XXVII

Old Home Day

Janet stood on the steps of the public library and stared at the minister with her mouth wide open.

"*Me?* Make a speech on Old Home Day?" she repeated.

"Yes. The committee wants you to tell the homecoming sons and daughters of Glenbrook what it's like to live in this village today."

"But Mr. Howells, I'm not the person to do that. Why don't you ask one of the girls or boys who've been in the high school debates or a college girl like Ethel Hayes?"

"I'll tell you why. We felt that you would put something into a speech that no other young person in this town could."

Slam! Slam! Slam! The books she had just taken out of the library dropped one by one. In her amazement, the girl had forgotten she had them under her arm.

"You will really have something to say and mean what you say," the minister went on when the books were back under Janet's arm. "You won't refuse us this favor, will you?"

It was terribly difficult to argue with Mr. Howells. She gave him five good reasons why she shouldn't speak for the young people of Glenbrook, and he came back with six reasons why she should. Arguing must be one of the things men had learned before they could be preachers, she decided. "At least," Janet comforted herself on the way home, "I have promised only to think it over."

Two weeks later, when programs for Glenbrook's first Old Home Day came from the printer, the name Janet Bradley was there, opposite the heading, "Growing Up in Glenbrook Today."

Every time the girl looked at her own name in print right after the name of the First Selectman and Nathan Phelps, the oldest graduate of Glenbrook Academy, and just before the governor of Massachusetts, she had cold chills.

Oh, the hours and days spent in preparing that speech! First, she wrote it all out. Then, she wrote most of it over again. After that came the memorizing it, then rehearsing.

Molly and her father grew quite used to having Janet almost anywhere or at any time suddenly stand very straight, assume a wooden expression, and begin, "Sons and Daughters of Glenbrook," in a voice that did not sound at all like her own. She tried speaking from the hayloft to see if her father could hear her at the other end of the barn, then recited from the buttery doorway while her father stood in the woodshed.

"You know that so well, you could say it in your sleep," Mr. Bradley reassured her. "And as for folks hearing you, I believe your voice must carry clear to the Warrens'."

Still the girl kept on going over and over her speech.

"You've got to have a new best dress if you're going to stand up on a platform and make a speech," wrote Grandma Williams.

A few days later, the old lady arrived with a large package of lawn and a small package of narrow lace. She spent three days on Laurel Hill cutting, basting, tucking, and gathering lengths of the crisp white material, adjusting the bertha and hanging the full skirt. When it was finished to the last bit of lace edging and Janet stood up for inspection, Grandma almost burst with pride. "You'll do!" she said.

Not in the memory of the town's oldest inhabitants had Glenbrookers been so excited as they were over plans for Old Home Day. News that this one and that one had accepted the invitation sent the flames of excitement mounting higher and higher, like branches thrown one by one on a bonfire. Judge Hopkins, whom Glenbrook had not seen for a quarter of a century, was traveling all the way from Chicago. The report that the governor might be present set young folks as well as old to rejoicing and swelling with pride. Why, it would be like Governor's Day at the Northbrook Cattle Show! There wouldn't be chairs enough in the whole town to seat all the crowd that would turn out! Janet exulted to Stephen.

"Pooh!" scoffed the boy, who was now getting about on crutches. "The governor won't come to a little place like this. You wait and see. He just wrote that he expected to spend August at his summer home in Stoneham, and that he *hoped* to be able to accept our kind invitation, and that we would hear from him again just as soon as his own plans were settled, and so forth, and so forth. Leaving himself a nice little hole to slip out of, isn't he?"

"Somehow I just know he'll be here," maintained Janet stoutly. She couldn't tell why she felt so sure of the governor, but this was the first big homecoming ever held in Glenbrook, and it seemed to her that anybody who was invited would make a special effort to be there.

"You can laugh all you want to, Steve, but I bet you a quarter he'll come."

"If the governor of the Commonwealth of Massachusetts so much as drives through this town this summer, I'll give you a two-pound box of the best chocolates money can buy."

"Two pounds! My, but you're rash, Steve!"

On the day before the great celebration, Glenbrookers waited anxiously for the weather report to come over the telephone at noon.

Great was the relief when Central announced that the morrow would be fair.

"And yet, you never can tell about dog days," said the farmers.

The report was confirmed for the Bradleys when the clouds above Laurel Hill glowed that evening, red as the coals in the kitchen range.

"Red sky at night, sailors' delight," quoted Janet.

Next morning, the sky was as blue as the morning glory blossoms reaching up to the porch roof to catch trumpetfuls of sunlight. The few clouds were of the harmless cotton-wool variety.

In an amazingly short time, the morning chores indoors and out were done. Then out of the closet came white dresses and Hamburg-trimmed petticoats that crackled with starch. Mr. Bradley put on a "biled shirt," Sunday suit with a cutaway coat, and the red-spotted necktie Molly had given him.

By the time Nancy had reached the bottom of the hill and the great buttonball tree that was the halfway mark between the Center and the Bradley farm, the drums of the Glenbrook fife and drum corps and the Eastbrook brass band, hired for the occasion, were heard thump-thumping away like a whole woods full of partridges. "Listen!" cried Molly, whose ears were sharp as a fox's. First Janet, then Mr. Bradley, caught the dull rub-a-dub-dub.

Not even on the biggest Fourth of July celebration in the town's history had there been so many people crowded into the center of Glenbrook as on this first Old Home Day. Every Glenbrooker who could climb in and out of a wagon had come. Ex-Glenbrookers were there—two trainloads of them. Eastbrook and Northbrook were represented in large numbers, lured by the news that the governor was going to speak. There was scarcely a vacant horse shed or barn or hitching post within a quarter of a mile of the Academy Green. The guests filled not only all the chairs and benches that had been placed on the green but also the academy steps, the town hall steps, and the steps and lawns of both churches. The sound of their mingled voices rising and falling was like a gust of wind passing over a great grove of trees.

When everyone stood up and sang "America," Janet felt sure that she could have heard that great wave of sound had she been on the tiptop of Laurel Hill. Now heads began turning toward the road and back at the clock on the meetinghouse steeple. Wasn't the governor coming? Selectman Hayes, chairman of the Welcoming Committee, looked worried as he rose to say a few words of greeting. Then, in the middle of a sentence, his face cleared. The cloppety-clop of fast-trotting horses sounded just above the post office, and in a moment a shiny carriage drawn by sleek, high-headed horses was rolling up to the edge of the green. At the sight of the man in the carriage, a great cheer rose.

Molly could not take her eyes off the glistening top hat the governor lifted high and waved. Next Christmas, she would buy a hat like that for Papa, no matter if it cost as much as a dollar.

Janet stole a triumphant glance at Stephen.

Chapter XXVIII

Janet Forgets Her Speech

The girl in the new white dress who sat beside Mr. Bradley and Molly kept swallowing an imaginary frog in her throat and crossing and uncrossing her legs. The new lace-edged handkerchief in her clammy hands had long since turned into a damp ball. "I'm next," she thought as Mr. Phelps rose to give his talk on "Glenbrook Fifty Years Ago." In a few minutes, it would be her turn to climb up on that bunting-draped platform and talk to all these people. Why, she'd do well just to get up the steps. Her legs felt like rubber legs, just the way they had the time she was so sick with scarlet fever. And suppose she forgot her speech! Pulling some folded sheets of paper out of the pocket in her skirt, Janet began reading over the familiar words once more.

All at once, she stopped reading, leaned forward, and began listening to the old man on the platform. What a lively place Glenbrook had been half a century ago! Stephen could never have called it a "dead hole" then. Boys and girls had come here from miles around to go to school. The old academy was famous. Great men had lectured in Academy Hall. And how much fun Glenbrookers had been in those days! There were singing schools, debating clubs, amateur theatricals, and other entertainments at the academy, and all sorts of "bees" at people's houses. She would like to go to one of those old-time cornhuskings or a barn raising or a quilting bee. Why in the world shouldn't life in Glenbrook be more interesting today and more fun?

She was roused from these thoughts by Molly nudging her anxiously and whispering, "That's you!"

"Our next speaker—" Joe Hayes, the chairman, had begun.

Janet smoothed the wrinkles out of her dress; patted the crisp, white-ribbon bow on her hair; and walked up the steps to where Joe Hayes; the minister; the great Judge Hopkins, Glenbrook's most famous son; and the governor sat like a board of examiners waiting to see if she could pass. She felt small and insignificant. The speech that had sounded wonderful at home in the kitchen and in the barn seemed utterly unimportant now—just words put together. If only she could speak right out and say some of the things on her mind! Mr. Phelps had set her to thinking, thinking hard! She came to a dead stop. Whatever was next? All the last part of that carefully memorized talk had gone out of her mind. It was just as if the words had been written on a slate, and a damp cloth had passed over them. She slid her hand into her pocket, then went cold all over. The precious paper wasn't there! It must have slipped from her lap that last time she took it out.

Never, so long as she lived, would Janet forget that moment of awful silence. It seemed like a half hour. She looked at Molly and her father and saw agonized expressions coming into their faces. "Say *something*. You've got to," she commanded herself. "Don't just stand here."

"Something has gone out of the life of this town since those days fifty years ago we've been hearing about," she heard herself saying. "Boys and girls are leaving Glenbrook and going to the towns and cities as fast as they can. Just one room of that old academy is used now—for a grammar school. That's as much schooling as you can get in Glenbrook. Until today, no famous men have come here to talk to us within memory of us young people. The worst of it is that a lot of the boys and girls who go to cities hate city life when they get there."

The girl hesitated and then began telling a little of her own story. She too had been discontented and had wanted—oh, how she had wanted!—to go to normal school or college. Then a way to do something interesting right here had been pointed out to her. She believed that other boys and girls could find ways of using their talents in the country if they only knew how. The trouble was they didn't hear enough about the possibilities of country life. They didn't have enough fun either—not half enough. Couldn't anything be done about it?

The chairman cleared his throat. That was the signal agreed upon in case she ran over the ten minutes allotted to her. There was a hint of disapproval in that rasping sound in Mr. Hayes' throat, she thought.

"We must put back into country life some of the things that we've lost. We must prove to young people that they don't have to go away to find either worthwhile work or fun," she ended hurriedly.

"Oh dear!" Janet said to herself as she went back to her seat. "I've put my foot in it, criticizing Glenbrook today before all these people." The applause was certainly not loud or enthusiastic. Some of the town's leading citizens looked positively glum. One thing Janet did not see, for it was behind her, was the governor's face. It was crinkled into smiles, and he was clapping as if he didn't care whether he blistered his hands or not. She did notice that one of the longest and loudest handclappers was Stephen. Just like him to try to make up for what the others didn't do. But how serious he looked. He seemed to be thinking hard about something.

To the girl's surprise, her father was no longer sitting on the bench beside her place. Was he ashamed of her speech?

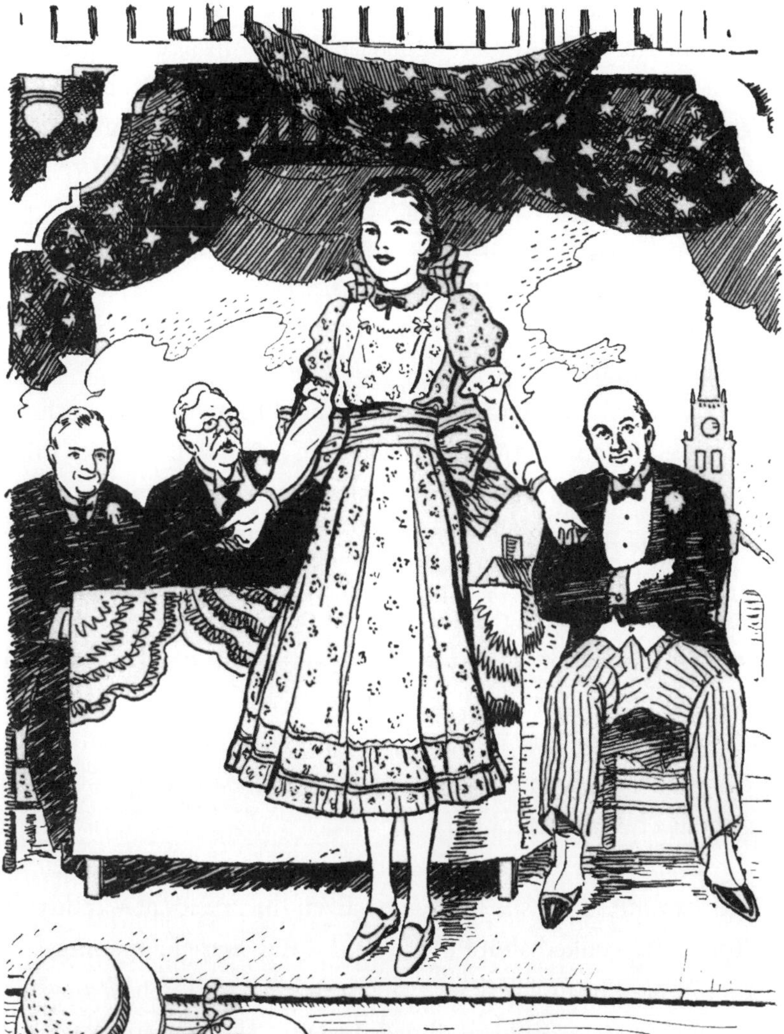

"Where's Papa?" she whispered to Molly.

The little girl smiled as if that were a secret.

Now came the big event of Old Home Day—the governor's speech. There was a tremendous rustle and stir as everyone rose and clapped a long, loud greeting. The great man bowed graciously and told them how happy he was "to be in one of the oldest and one of the most beautiful towns in the entire Commonwealth," then announced to the amazement of all present, "The young lady who just spoke from this platform has an old head on young shoulders."

"He means *you*, Janet," whispered Molly, as if doubting the governor's sanity.

"While listening to her, I decided not to make the speech I prepared for this occasion. Instead, I'm going to talk about this problem of making country life worthwhile and attractive so that young people will want to stay in towns like Glenbrook."

Bright pink spots glowed in Janet's cheeks. Everybody seemed to be looking at her and whispering things to each other about her. In a minute, she was oblivious of all except the man on the platform, not wanting to miss a word he said. Her eyes opened wider and wider. People all over the state, all over the country, it seemed, were taking an interest in boys and girls like her and Stephen.

In the State House in Boston, men were trying to answer the very questions she had asked. Even the president—Teddy Roosevelt—talked about them. And things were happening, too. At agricultural colleges, men were discovering new ways of making farms pay and of making country life more fun and were passing on their discoveries. Farmers and farmers' wives were waking up to the possibilities of life in a village like Glenbrook. "Like your Miss Bradley," the governor said, "they often find unused and unsuspected treasure right on their own land."

At this point, there was a furious nudging from Molly.

The great man ceased speaking, acknowledged the tumult of cheers and clapping with a deep bow, shook hands with Joe Hayes, and was escorted by two leading citizens to his carriage. He deeply regretted, and so did everyone else, especially the good cooks of Glenbrook, that he could not stay for the dinner on the green.

Before dinner could be served, there was one more speaker to be heard from—the judge who had come back to his birthplace all the way from Chicago. People cheered him as loudly as they had the governor, and most people liked his speech better than the governor's. He told more funny stories, and his boyhood memories were a delight to all the older people.

Janet's attention wandered. Then she heard her own name spoken once more from the platform and felt a sharp poke from Molly's elbow.

Good heavens! The judge was asking her to come up on the platform and answer a question, and the question was, "What would you do for Glenbrook if you had a thousand dollars?"

With a thousand dollars! What wouldn't she do? Gone were the rubber legs. Gone was the frog in her throat. This time, she fairly bounded up the steps and onto the platform.

"First, I'd use part of it to send to Eastbrook High School those bright boys and girls who want to go on after they've finished grammar school here and can't afford to because they're needed at home or can't pay railroad fare or something. Why shouldn't they have as good a chance for an education today as they had fifty years ago? Then I'd offer a prize every year to the boy and the girl who wrote the best essays on 'Why I Like to Live on a Farm,' and the prizes would be scholarships for a year's tuition at Massachusetts Agricultural College. Next, I'd clean up and paint up old Academy Hall and use it. I'd get together the folks who like to sing and start a Glenbrook Glee

Club and hire a music teacher to come and teach them. Then, I'd get somebody that knew about putting on plays to coach the dramatic club, that is, if folks wanted a dramatic club—and—and—there'd be a lot of other things just the way there used to be years ago."

The judge grinned. "Aren't you spending more than a thousand dollars, young lady?" he asked.

"Oh no, I don't think so," the girl assured him earnestly. "You see, we'd all get together and clean and paint the hall ourselves, so that wouldn't cost us much, and we'd charge admission to our plays and concerts, and that's how we'd pay for the music teacher and the coach and so on. I just know I could do an awful lot with a thousand dollars, Judge Hopkins."

"By Jove! I believe you could," the great man agreed heartily.

When Janet left the platform this time, people clapped as if they meant it. Even after she was back on the bench beside Molly, the applause went on. "That Bradley girl's smart as a whip," whispered Glenbrookers who had never paid any attention to her before. Even Joe Hayes looked impressed. A girl singled out by the governor and the judge for praise must be smart.

Judge Hopkins called for suggestions from the audience for improving Glenbrook, and to Janet's amazement, the first one on his feet was Stephen. "I didn't know until I heard the governor's talk how much there was to farming and what interesting things there were to learn at agricultural schools," he announced. "I think we ought to ask Massachusetts 'Aggie' to send some of their teachers here next winter and hold one of those institutes he was telling us about."

Laughter mingled with the clapping when Billy Hastings said he'd had to go clear up to the Klondike and back and freeze his ears and most of his fingers 'fore he learned that there "wasn't no flies on Glenbrook." The only trouble was boys and girls didn't have enough fun. If he had a thousand dollars, he'd spend most of it giving the young folks good times. That was the best way to keep them on the farms.

Presently, people were jumping up all over the green to say what they thought should be done or not be done for Glenbrook. It was like a town meeting. There's no telling how long all this talk would have gone on if Joe Hayes had not pounded the table with the town clerk's gavel and roared that the ladies were ready to serve dinner just as soon as room was made on the green for the tables.

Janet was almost in a daze as she rose and followed the crowd to the edge of the square. Her cheeks blazed with excitement. So much had happened to her so quickly, yet the day's surprises were not over. If she had been watching her father when he got up and left his seat, she would have seen that he had gone to meet a lady who had just arrived and was waving to him from the edge of the green. As it was, this surprise was complete. Not until she had walked almost into her arms did the girl see Cousin Anna. Then she gave a squeal of joy that could have been heard for a mile. "How ever did you get here?" she wanted to know.

"On the eleven o'clock train. When your father wrote and sent us a copy of the program, I said I was coming to hear you talk, Janet, if I had to walk all the way, and here I am."

Once or twice in a lifetime, a perfect day happens. This was one of those days for Janet Bradley.

Chapter XXIX

"You've Grown Up, Janet"

"Sakes alive! I never did see a girl grow up in two years like you have, never."

It was the day after Old Home Day. Cousin Anna sat talking with Janet on the porch. Molly played with paper dolls on the broad doorstone, silent as a little stone image but missing no word of the conversation.

The older girl set down the pan of pole beans she was shelling, jumped up, and stood as tall as possible against one of the posts of the porch. Marking with a finger the place where the top of her head came, she whirled around and looked closely at some pencil marks lower down. "I've grown three inches since you saw me before, and I'm an inch taller than Mamma was," she announced proudly.

At this point, Molly, of course, had to measure herself and report that she was four inches taller than she was two years ago.

"Yes, you've both shot up," agreed their cousin, "but I wasn't thinking of that kind of growing. You've grown up inside, Janet."

"I feel happier inside."

"You would, because you've changed from a sorry-for-herself child into a young lady who is quite capable of looking after herself and of bringing up a younger sister and is even willing to take on the job of helping the whole town."

They both laughed.

"You make me sound terrible—plain and stout and managing everybody—with a hatchet in my hand like Carrie Nation."

Anna Bates looked at the slim girl beside her and smiled. "I wouldn't lie awake at night worrying about being plain and stout if I were you, and I'm pretty sure you don't."

The eighteen-year-old and the middle-aged woman had much to talk about. Beginning with the exciting developments on the green the day before, they worked backward, living over the two years since Janet and Molly had watched the hill road for the appearance of those mysterious cousins from Redfield. They compared notes on their businesses and on the way life had treated them in general.

"Do you know what I said to myself yesterday when I listened to you talking up there on the platform?" Cousin Anna asked.

"Couldn't guess."

"I said, 'The last time I saw that girl, she was a-worrying and a-stewing for fear she'd grow up into an ignoramus, and just look at her now—making the governor himself sit up and take notice.' I almost laughed out loud at the very idea."

"No, I'm not an ignoramus," Janet agreed. "I've studied hard at home, and the Roaring Brook School teacher has been coaching me right along. I can do the hard problems in geometry and algebra now, and I've read *Caesar* and *Cicero* and two French books and almost all the required reading for college entrance. I guess you were right that time when you said that a person could get an education even if he couldn't go to school much."

So busy were they talking, they did not hear hoofbeats or a clear whistle till Stephen, riding up the hill on Fan's back, was almost in the yard. Having tied the horse to a hitching post, he produced a box from under his arm and, bowing low with mock ceremony, presented it to Janet.

"You won," he explained briefly.

"And I thought you'd forgotten all about that bet."

"Me! I'm not that kind of fellow."

"Why Steve Warren, it's Rogers and Hyde's! Assorted chocolates! Where did you get them?"

"Took a little trip to Eastbrook last evening. I figured the best was none too good for the star of Old Home Day. Sa-ay, I hear Joe Hayes is going to resign so's they can make you First Selectman, or rather First Selectwoman."

His voice suddenly lost its teasing quality. "Honest, Janet, you were wonderful yesterday. Folks down at the Center are saying the judge is going to do something handsome for this town. If he does, we'll have you to thank."

The girl was skeptical. "It's probably all talk. Anyway, we can do a whole lot of things for ourselves."

"You betcha."

Whirring wheels and tinkling bells announced the arrival of Delia and Roy on their bicycles.

"What do you think I've decided to do?" asked Delia, popping into her mouth a chocolate nougat from Janet's box. "That is, after I've been to the Conservatory of Music?"

"Marry one of your teachers," suggested her brother.

"Not on your life. Music teachers are always cross. I planned it all out yesterday, after Janet's speech—the second one. I'll teach music in Eastbrook and come back here and teach those musical clubs we're going to have here. And wouldn't it be simply wonderful if all our crowd could stay around here and do some of those things you and the governor talked about yesterday, Janet, and never be separated from one another?" In her excitement, Delia bit into a tinfoil-wrapped chocolate without removing the wrapping.

"It would be wonderful, all right," agreed Janet.

"Maybe I'll be a dairy farmer instead of a banker," said Roy. "Still and all, I guess I'd better try out banking as long as a job's waiting for me and I've been and taken a business course. Anyway, Northbrook's so near, I can come home every Sunday."

"Let's all settle down on the farm," suggested Stephen mockingly. "I've heard tell that cities are mighty wicked places, and a boy can't go wrong if he stays with the cows."

Janet flashed a scornful look at him. "Perhaps the cows would object to some folks' staying with them." Why did Steve always have to make fun of farm life? It did not occur to her that he was trying hard not to show how much he too wished that all four of them might stay forever in Glenbrook.

"Hey!" called Hiram Austen loudly as he drove up to the mailbox, "you've got your name in the paper, Janet." He waved in the air a copy of the *Eastbrook Gazette*.

Instantly, the porch was empty. Molly, who had long since retired behind the lilac bush, emerged, followed by the dog.

GLENBROOK GIRL CALLS VILLAGE TO ACTION
"Make Country Life More Interesting," She Says

Stephen, who had been the first to reach the mailbox, read out the headlines while the others looked over his shoulders. "Lookit, Janet, there's almost half a column about you, and even the governor only got a column." He gave a long expressive whistle.

"What's that about the judge over there at the left?" asked the girl.

"'Judge Hopkins offers to establish a fund for an experiment in country life improvement.' Jiminy Cricket!"

Mr. Bradley, hearing excited voices, came from the potato field and wanted to know what was going on.

"Your gal's started something; I dunno just what," said Hiram, continuing reluctantly on his way.

"Now," suggested Cousin Anna when they were back on the porch, "if everybody'll sit down and keep quiet, I'll read the paper out loud. We can't all see it at once, that's certain."

"Seems as if it was about some other girl," was Janet's comment after listening to the report of her own talk.

"Sounds just exactly like you in one of your earnest moods," Stephen assured her.

"That's a fact," agreed Roy.

"'Janet Bradley—a pretty, dark-haired, dark-eyed girl,'" repeated Delia ecstatically. "Just imagine being called pretty in the newspaper!"

Molly said not a word. What a lot of fuss over nothing much! She could have written an original poem for the occasion and recited it, if anybody had asked her to. Never had being a younger sister seemed quite so unsatisfactory. She slipped a large chocolate peppermint into her mouth and immediately felt somewhat better. Then, putting a caramel in the pocket of her pinafore, she went back behind the lilac bush.

It was hard to tell which was in greater danger of bursting with pride—Cousin Anna or Mr. Bradley. Both were quiet for a few minutes after the reading was over. Then the girl's father gave a deep chuckle. "Yes, it looks like you'd started something, Janet."

Chapter XXX

Stephen Changes His Mind

Once again, the maples and sumac glowed like bright banners against the pines on Laurel Hill. Again, the voice of Etta Hastings announced joyously—

> *"We shall come, rejoicing,*
> *Bringing in the sheaves."*

"Somehow I always feel just like singing that hymn when I see folks bringing in the laurel and ferns," she said.

The woodshed was fragrant with the smell of the woods and was humming with women's voices. Up through the frost-browned fields went a slim, red-capped girl. There were plenty of other people to gather green treasure for Janet. Yet every now and then, no matter how busy she was in her shop, she had to run away to the woods and have the fun of picking the laurel and ferns and pine for herself.

Never had this brown-carpeted, green-roofed room seemed more beautiful than on this October day. "It's already decorated for Christmas," thought the girl, noticing how the bittersweet and the red alder berries looked as if someone had hung a vine here or stuck a bunch there where it would show off to the best advantage.

When she leaned over the spring to drink, she had to clear away the bright yellow leaves that had fallen from the beech tree. Looking at the golden disks made Janet laugh softly to herself. Those childhood dreams of finding a gold mine or buried treasure on Laurel Hill had come true after all—partly true anyway. Green treasure hadn't made her rich, but it had provided a good many extras for herself and Molly and Papa, and the work had brought her much happiness. She had created beauty, and it seemed to her that those who created beauty must always be happy.

The girl sat down for a few minutes under the great pine tree by the spring and indulged in a little solid self-satisfaction. She had launched a successful business on Laurel Hill—probably the last place where anybody would expect a business would flourish.

"Say it," she told herself, laughing out loud, "you think you're pretty smart, don't you?

"'Course I do. I'll bet not many girls my age get asked to be trustees."

Hadn't the judge appointed her along with the First Selectman, the minister, and the chairman of the school committee to be a trustee of the Amos Hopkins Fund? Already some of her own ideas were being carried out. The academy building had been painted inside and out, and new seats had been bought for the hall to replace the old broken benches, also new lamps. The Glenbrook Choral Society was making the old building ring with songs. Plans were underway for all sorts of activities, both serious and frivolous.

As a trustee of the fund, Janet knew a secret she couldn't tell anybody. Two boys and a girl—all three as bright as gold dollars—were going to the Eastbrook High School this fall, young folks who couldn't have gone on if it hadn't been for the judge's fund. Yes, she really had started something that day she had said what was on her mind to the Old Home Day crowd.

Dick, who lay stretched out at his mistress' feet, cocked a

silky ear and gave a quick bark followed by a subdued *woof*, as if to say, "Someone's coming. But it's all right—a friend." The friend was singing in a loud voice—

> *"If you lak-a-me*
> *Lak I lak-a-you*
> *And we lak-a-both the same,*
> *I lak-a-say this very day*
> *I lak-a-change your name."*

"It's Steve," the girl told the listening dog, as if Dick's nose and ears hadn't notified him who was coming long before she knew.

"Hello, Janet. Thought I'd find you here. When nobody knows where you are, I always look up here in the woods."

He dropped down beside her on the pine needles.

"I'm glad you changed your mind—about not coming home till November," she told him.

"I've changed my mind about a number of things. I came home this week especially to tell you what I've done. It just wouldn't keep till November. And you couldn't guess, Janet, not if I gave you ten guesses." His eyes held the twinkle that always meant he was about to spring a tremendous surprise.

"Stop working up suspense and tell me."

"All right. Take a deep breath. I'm not going to Amherst College anymore. I'm going to Massachusetts Aggie."

"Wha-at? What did you say?"

Stephen repeated what he had just said.

"Since when?"

"Ever since the beginning of college, but I wrote the folks to keep it under their hats till I came home. I wanted to see how you looked when you heard the news."

"Did I look the way you expected me to?"

"Yes, but your eyes got even bigger, and your mouth opened wider. By the way, don't you think you've left your mouth open long enough?"

The girl shut it with a sharp click of her teeth. "Now, Steve Warren, will you *please* tell me how you happened to do it after all your talk about hating farms—and so suddenly?"

"This isn't really as sudden as you think, Janet. I began changing my mind last July, only I wouldn't admit it for a long time even to myself. You see, while I was laid up with that broken ankle, I did a lot of thinking about the past, present, and future. It struck me like a lightning bolt one day that I was planning to spend most of my life shut up indoors, and that I'd hate it.

"Then Old Home Day made me use my gray matter some more—especially what you said. I hadn't ever stopped to think before about those things—how this place didn't need to be a dead hole for a fellow with any gumption, that you and I and all of us could have interesting lives here in Glenbrook. 'Say, Steve,' I said, 'wake up and hear the birdies sing. You've been sound asleep.'

"The governor, he made me sit up and take notice, too. By the time he was through, I could see that there was a whole lot more to this business of farming than I'd had any idea—new ways of doing things and new kinds of things to do.

"Honestly, Janet, were you talking about me that day—Old Home Day?"

"About you? Why, no."

"Well, it seemed like you *meant* me when you said lots of country boys were dead sure they wanted jobs in the city and then hated it all after they got there. 'You're one of those fellows, Steve, old boy,' I told myself. 'You'll be a fish out of water, all right.' But I was bound I wouldn't let you know what a jolt you'd given me."

He was silent for a few moments, then added, "Of course, the hardest jolt I got that day was just getting on to what you've made of yourself, Janet. By jiminy, you've shown what a girl can do right here, even when she had to drop out in the middle of high school. And to think that I accused you of not being ambitious! You've been as ambitious as any of us and a—a bigger person."

The red-capped girl leaning against the tree trunk was almost reduced to speechlessness. "W-why, Steve," she stammered, then she burst out laughing, "you certainly concealed your admiration from me. I never suspected it."

"I haven't half told you yet what I think about you." His eyes met hers and said what his lips couldn't manage to say.

"When did you decide to go Aggie?" she asked quickly.

"Not till I was back in Amherst and had my things unpacked and my room all fixed up. Then I began to feel like I didn't belong there, not with the fellows who were going to be lawyers and bankers and schoolteachers. So I sneaked off and got an Aggie catalog and stuck my nose in it for a while. I guess it was those courses in horticulture and that new course they're giving in forestry that cinched it with me, those and a talk I had with a professor over there. He seemed to know just how I was feeling—kind of pulled two ways—and he let me sit and talk to him till I knew myself what I wanted to do. And now, what do you think about it all, Janet? You haven't told me."

"If what you really want to be is an up-to-the-minute farmer, I think it's the best news I've heard for years and years."

"You bet I do, only I'm going to specialize in the kind of farming I like. I'm going to learn how to take care of our woodland and how to grow new timber and about the bugs that kill trees and how to prevent forest fires and fight them and how to take care of orchards. You've no idea how much there is to learn about all those things.

"There's another reason why I changed my mind about being a college professor." He began talking very fast, as if afraid the girl might try to stop him. "You see, colleges are usually in towns, at least the big colleges, and I don't think you'd ever like living in a town. As a matter of fact, I can't quite picture you living anywhere except on top of a hill looking off to other hills, and with pine woods somewhere around."

"What have *I* got to do with it?" Janet knew perfectly well the answer to her question.

"Everything. That's all—just everything."

Janet had never seen Stephen look so terribly in earnest before.

"You see," he went on, talking fast again, "I've got a wonderful plan, but it's going to take both of us to carry it out. When I'm finished at Aggie, I want to come home and put what I've learned to use right here—helping Pa run the sawmill, replanting cutover woodland, starting a tree nursery and a new apple orchard. Then, after I'm going good and Molly's big enough to get along without you—say three or four years from now—I'll build a house for you and me on Halfway Knoll. If you want to go on with your business, you can, and if my nursery does well, there'll be Christmas trees to sell as well as wreaths and things. Oh! Janet, together we can lick our weight in wildcats. I know we can."

He stopped and looked at her, hoping to read her thoughts. The girl kept her eyes on the spray of ground pine with which her fingers played.

"Don't you like my plan? Don't you want to be part of it?" His voice begged to be answered immediately.

Her smile was almost answer enough. "Like it! I can't think of a single improvement for your plan, Steve. It's perfect. I'm glad," she added, "that we're planning our future here. Dreams made in these woods come true."

Dick, sound asleep at his mistress' feet, gave a long, contented grunt, as if he knew exactly what was going on and was satisfied that all was well on Laurel Hill.

THE END

More Books from The Good and the Beautiful Library!

A Girl of the Limberlost
by Gene Stratton-Porter

Jacqueline of the Carrier Pigeons
by Augusta Huiell Seaman

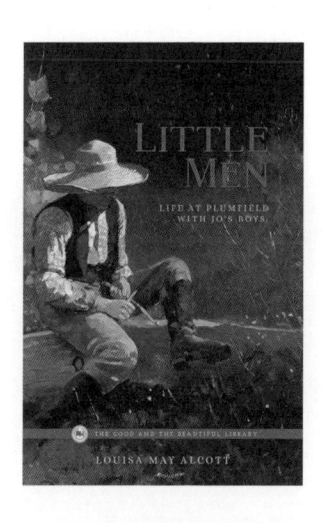

Little Men
by Louisa May Alcott

Dawn
by Eleanor H. Porter

www.thegoodandthebeautiful.com